A Slight Case of Mistaken Identity

He thinks... Sure, Mari Lamott may have been able to fool my grandmother with her phony psychic readings, but I'm an undercover detective, and my instincts are *never* wrong. Besides, that pink feather boa was all the proof I needed to make a positive ID. Still, I've never been one to resist a challenge—especially not one as pretty as Miss Lamott!

She thinks... Why does it seem as if I spend my entire life bailing my twin sister out of trouble? Thanks to her crazy antics, I'm masquerading as a psychic, spending more money on bail than I do on rent, and I've got a pink feather boa on my floor! Add to that chaos one sexy stranger who's taken a sudden interest in my every move and...well, let's just say it seems as if my boring life is finally starting to heat up!

Dear Reader,

I've never had a twin, but I can see how much fun it might be to have someone who looks just like you but leads a completely different life, a life you could share if the two of you decided to trade places for a while. For Mari Lamott, things are a bit more complicated than that, though. The heroine of Kelly Jamison's *The Law and Miss Lamott* has a twin who's nothing but trouble, so taking her place brings trouble in its wake. Of course, it also brings handsome detective Patrick Keegan—and getting together with a man that gorgeous is certainly worth a bit of trouble. Read this delightful book and see if you don't agree with me.

This month also brings the newest installment of award-winning Marie Ferrarella's latest miniseries, THE CUTLERS OF THE SHADY LADY RANCH. In *Will and the Headstrong Female* you can watch a rancher with a strong protective streak, Will Cutler, clash with an independent woman—Denise Cavanaugh—who comes driving into town intending to drive right out again once the carnival she runs is over. But somehow she ends up staying—and you'll be as glad as she is that she did.

Have fun with this month's selections, and don't forget to come back to Yours Truly next month for two more books about unexpectedly meeting—and marrying!—Mr. Right.

Yours,

Leslie J. Wainger
Executive Senior Editor

Please address questions and book requests to:
Silhouette Reader Service
U.S.: 3010 Walden Ave., P.O. Box 1325, Buffalo, NY 14269
Canadian: P.O. Box 609, Fort Erie, Ont. L2A 5X3

KELLY JAMISON

The Law and Miss Lamott

SILHOUETTE BOOKS

HARLEQUIN AW-AKO-KINBA-BANCHLE

Copyright 1997 by Jade Blackburn

All rights reserved. Except for use in any review, the reproduction or utilization of this work in whole or in part in any form by any electronic, mechanical or other means, now known or hereafter invented, including xerography, photocopying and recording, or in any information storage or retrieval system, is forbidden without the written permission of the publisher, Silhouette Books, 300 East 42nd Street, New York, N.Y. 10017 U.S.A.

All the characters in this book have no existence outside the imagination of the author and have no relation whatsoever to anyone bearing the same name or names. They are not even distantly inspired by any individual known or unknown to the author, and all the incidents are pure invention.

This edition published by arrangement with Harlequin Books S.A.

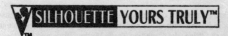

Published by Silhouette Books
America's Publisher of Contemporary Romance

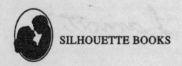

SILHOUETTE BOOKS

ISBN 0-373-52080-8

THE LAW AND MISS LAMOTT

Copyright © 1998 by Linda Buechting

Dear Reader,

Travel! Adventure! Excitement! Just like Mari Lamott, I dreamed of a more exciting life. I would live in Paris and write books and stay up all night painting. I would eat exotic foods and wear a hat every day just because I love hats.

Well, I do write books. But I do it from a small room on the second floor of my house in Illinois, looking out over my flower bed filled with foxgloves, hollyhocks and weeds, not from a small café on the banks of the Seine River in France. Usually I'm drinking a diet soda or tea and nibbling on jelly beans, not quite the champagne and truffles I pictured in my dreams.

I wear a hat now and then. But not often, because it's windy in Illinois. And I paint—but not all night.

All in all, I'm pretty darn happy. Maybe my dreams came true after all. Life has a funny habit of happening when you're not paying attention.

Best,

Kelly Jamison

P.S. If you would like some hollyhock seeds, write to Kelly Jamison, P.O. Box 5223, Quincy, Illinois 62305.

Books by Kelly Jamison

1

What does your future hold? Tarot cards, crystal ball and palm reading by certified psychic. I see it all. Call Mariette at 555-2144.

Mari Lamott—she refused to use her full name of Mariel, because people kept confusing her with her twin sister—didn't need a crystal ball to predict the potential disasters that Mariette's ad in the community newspaper might bring. Right on cue, the phone began ringing.

She groaned. When the ad appeared two days ago, on Friday, Mari fielded two calls. The first was from a woman who had all but promised to write her a hefty check if she could provide the winning lottery numbers. Mari had told her that if she knew the winning lottery numbers, did she really think she would be running an ad for psychic readings?

The second caller had wanted to know if she should break up with her boyfriend who had proposed the week before. Mari had tried to tell her that she wasn't a psychic, that the person who placed the ad was no longer at this address, but the caller wouldn't give up. Finally, in desperation, Mari told her that if she wasn't sure she wanted to marry her boyfriend, then maybe a wedding wasn't such a good idea. The woman had hung up in a huff.

Mari tried glaring at the phone, but it continued to ring.

Yesterday there was another call from a single woman who wanted a peek into her dating future. Mari had assured her that if she could predict romance, that would take all the fun out of it now, wouldn't it?

The phone was still ringing, and Mari gave in.

"Is this the psychic's number?" a thin voice asked.

"Yes—I mean no," Mari said. "It's the number in the ad, but there's no psychic here."

"Now, don't be modest, dear," the voice said, and Mari pictured a smiling, older woman. "You wouldn't have placed that ad if you didn't feel you had the calling."

"Oh, yes, I would," Mari muttered, thinking of her sister's past schemes to make money. This psychic thing was the latest in Mariette's string of harebrained attempts to liven up her bank account and her life. In the process, she usually complicated Mari's life while flattening Mari's bank account.

The woman chuckled. "A psychic with a sense of humor. I like that. I was wondering if you could come do a reading for me, dear."

"I'm afraid I'm not really in the psychic business." The truth of the matter was that right after placing the ad, Mariette had met a biker—the latest in a string of leather-clad, pierced and jobless boyfriends—and they had taken off together to explore the world from his Harley. His name was Harmon. As unfamiliar with motorcycles as she was with men, Mari had trouble remembering which name was the man and which was the motorcycle.

"Do you think you could come over this afternoon?" the woman asked. "I know it's short notice, but I could really use some advice. I'm worried about my grandchildren."

"Really, Mrs.—" Mari began.

"Keegan," the woman said. "Rose Keegan. I don't want to bother you, but it's just that..." She sighed. "I'm sorry. I'm acting like a lonely old woman, and I hate whiners."

"No, no," Mari said hastily. "I suppose it would be all right if I...come visit you." She couldn't bring herself to say that she would give a psychic reading. She wasn't a psychic, and what she knew about tarot cards and crystal balls would fit on a bubble gum wrapper. But, she also didn't have the heart to turn down an obviously lonely older woman. Mari played the piano once a week at a local nursing home, and she had seen loneliness at its worst.

"Oh, that's so nice of you," Rose Keegan exclaimed. "And I've got some fresh chocolate-chip cookies."

Mari smiled despite her qualms. Any calories consumed while performing a good deed didn't count; at least that was Mari's philosophy. "That sounds nice," she said.

So that was how she found herself pulling into Rose Keegan's driveway an hour later. She fully intended to tell the woman that she was no psychic, but that didn't explain why she had wrapped one of her sister's colorful scarves around her waist, right over the soft, flower-print peasant skirt. She had also put on a little white blouse with a big collar and, for a final touch, had fastened gold hoops at her ears. She couldn't change her chin-length, wavy brown hair or her brown eyes, for that matter, but she certainly looked more mysterious than usual.

She really intended to tell Rose Keegan the truth, but it wouldn't hurt to pretend just for the drive over that she was something other than mousy little Mari Lamott who usually wore sturdy shoes that were as dependable as she was. It was kind of fun pretending for a half hour anyway that she was the flashy sister, the one who led an exciting life. Pigeon Nook, Indiana, was a fairly small, conservative town that took life seriously. Having been born there and drunk the city water for all of her thirty years, Mari felt as ordinary and nondescript as the town itself. It might be fun to live on the edge for a day.

When Rose Keegan opened the door of the plain, white frame house, Mari caught the scent of her flowery cologne mingled with the aroma of fresh cookies. She immediately thought of her own grandmother who lived in a condo in Florida, far enough from Indiana that Mari only heard from her on holidays, and felt a pang of loneliness herself. It occurred to Mari that for a woman like her grandmother or Mrs. Keegan to consult a so-called psychic was a dangerous thing. Someone could so easily take advantage of an older woman who was alone.

"Well," Rose said, gesturing her inside. "Aren't you a sweet little thing? Now come have a seat and tell me about yourself."

"There's not much to tell," Mari said hesitantly,

taking a seat on one end of the floral-printed couch. The room was small and warm, the heat of August making her feel suddenly drowsy. She glanced around, noticing some framed photos on a doily-draped table beside the television. The room was painted a bright yellow, and she noticed that Rose Keegan was dressed brightly as well. Her pink dress had tiny blue daisies spashed all over it, and someone had painted a white daisy on the head of the cane that now rested beside her chair.

"Are there other psychics in your family, dear?" Rose asked companionably.

"Yes—I mean no," Mari said, realizing that this was the second time she had stumbled over one of Rose's questions. "I mean, some of us in my family tend to see into the future a lot better than others." That certainly wasn't a lie. There were dozens of times when Mari could have told her sister that she was going to get into trouble, but Mariette always failed to see the warning signs in time.

"I see." Rose appeared about to ask another question when a man's voice called through the screen door.

"You aren't doing anything illegal in there, are you, Gram?"

Mari jumped when she saw a man silhouetted against the screen, his hand cupped to his forehead as he looked inside. She could see that he was tall and well built, and his voice had been definitely masculine and teasing.

"Come on in, Patrick," Rose called. "I was just about to bring out some chocolate-chip cookies, if you want to call that unlawful."

"They do come pretty close to a mind-altering substance," the man said playfully as he stepped inside.

His eyes did a quick once-over on Mari, and she found herself flushing under his scrutiny. The smile was still on his face, but it didn't escape her notice that his eyes were suddenly wary. And nice eyes they were. If you happened to like a lush green shade that made his blond hair look all the more striking. Mari felt a sizzling in her blood that had nothing to do with August heat.

"Dear, this is Mariette," Rose said, gesturing toward the couch. "Mariette, this is my grandson, Patrick. Patrick Keegan."

"Nice to meet you," Mari said, frowning as she held out her hand and it was swallowed in a much larger, harder one. "And, please. Everyone calls me Mari." She didn't think she could stammer out an explanation of who she really was while Patrick Keegan was watching her with those intense eyes. She would just have to make her escape as quickly as possible and explain things to Rose later. "I should be going," she said, making a motion to stand.

"Oh, but you haven't done my reading yet," Rose said in disappointment.

"Reading?" Patrick asked, and Mari heard the suspicion in his voice.

"Mariette—Mari—was going to do a psychic reading for me, dear," Rose said. "Now don't go, Mari, honey, until you have some cookies."

"By all means," Patrick said dryly, his eyes returning to Mari. "Stay for the cookies."

Mari didn't like the look in his eyes as Rose went to get the cookies. She fully intended to leave as soon as possible, but she was having a little trouble marshaling her thoughts the way this intimidating man continued to watch her.

He was wearing jeans and a black T-shirt, and now he stuck his hands into his pockets, still standing.

"What kind of psychic readings do you do, Mari?" he asked, and, looking up at him, Mari thought she understood how a mouse felt when cornered by a cat. He must be a little over six feet tall, and she felt dwarfed at a hair under five foot five.

She swallowed and shrugged. "Nothing really." When his brows went up challengingly, she tried to improvise. "Maybe a little tarot cards, my crystal ball."

"Which you don't seem to have with you," he said with mock disappointment.

"I was actually planning on reading your grandmother's palm," Mari said, wishing she didn't have this stubborn streak that compelled her to finish everything she started, even when what she started was clearly not working out.

"How interesting," he said, a brief smile tugging up one corner of his mouth as his grandmother came back with a plate of cookies. "Sit down, Gram, and let our little psychic read your palm. This should be entertaining."

There was that challenge in his voice again. It made Mari want to grab her purse and run for the door, but she didn't. She liked Rose Keegan, although her grandson was more than a little intimidating. Obviously he thought she was some wacko nitwit who passed herself off as a psychic. Well, she would give him a performance he wouldn't forget. She'd seen enough guests on the "Sally Jesse Raphael" and "Montel Williams" TV shows to know how wacko nitwits acted. Not to mention her sister.

Mari took one of the cookies Rose offered and nibbled it thoughtfully.

"I normally do readings when I'm a little more...in a trance," she said, "but I'll do what I can."

Mari finished her cookie, then sat with a flourish on the hassock in front of Rose's chair. Patrick, still standing, now moved to her side.

"Not so close," Mari warned imperiously. "You're ruining my vibrations." She waved him away, and he retreated a few steps, an amused smile on his face.

Momentarily bolstered by her newfound bravado, Mari took Rose's hand in hers and turned it palm up. She pretended to study it, trying to remember any of the things her sister had said when she did a practice run on Mari. But, at the time, Mari had been too busy explaining to Mariette why this latest scheme wasn't going to make her rich to take in any details of Mariette's prattle.

"My, but you have a lovely life line," Mari said at last. She started to trace the line, then stopped as she realized she had no idea exactly which one was the life line. "Let's see what your family line has to say."

"Family line?" Patrick asked dryly.

Mari shushed him. "You're breaking my concentration," she complained. She heard him sigh impatiently, and she hurried on. "Yes, you have children." *Great, Mari,* she thought. *Anybody would know that.*

Remembering the photos on the table, Mari pressed the back of one hand to her forehead as if concentrating, then peeked sideways. She could make out what looked like a family photo with Rose surrounded by several young men. Grandchildren? She couldn't be sure. There was one of Patrick in the midst of boys in baseball uniforms, one smiling kid holding up a trophy.

Mari cleared her throat. "You love children." That seemed safe enough. "So does your grandson. I see him surrounded by boys." She pretended to concentrate harder. "Boys who love sports. No, one special sport. Wait, it's coming to me. Baseball!" She heard Patrick snort derisively but ignored him. Another peek at the pictures showed a single photo of some big, bearded guy in a tank top with a sweatband around his forehead and one earring. She suspected that Rose was a fan. But of what? Obviously the guy wasn't a chess champion.

"Rose, you like sports, too," she began tentatively. "You're especially fond of one young man in a special sport. He's big, and he wears—" she paused dramatically "—an earring." She waited, hoping Rose would provide a clue, but Patrick cleared his throat. Now what sport required big, beefy guys? Rose's hand closed on Mari's, and she knew Rose was giving her silent encouragement. Mari was beginning to hear the theme of "Final Jeopardy" in her head.

"I can see this is going nowhere," Patrick said in disgust.

It came to Mari in a flash. Opening her eyes, she lifted her head and cried, "Professional wrestling! She loves to watch wrestlers!"

There was a startled silence before Patrick began to laugh. "Professional wrestling?" he repeated incred-

ulously. He began to laugh harder, and when Mari
glanced at Rose she saw that she was smiling, as well.

Rose patted Mari's hand. "I believe you're thinking
of my grandson, honey," she said kindly. "Patrick's
cousin. Elroy Keegan. He's a chef."

A chef. And she'd called him a wrestler. Deciding
that she'd humiliated herself about as much as she
could for one day, Mari rose with all the dignity she
could muster.

She thanked Rose for the cookies and started for the
door, determined to ignore Patrick Keegan.

"But I haven't paid you yet!" Rose cried.

"Oh, no, I couldn't accept any money," Mari said
firmly. "It was my pleasure just to visit."

Rose started to protest, but Patrick interrupted. "I'm
sure your cookies more than compensated Mari for her
psychic talents," he said smoothly.

Mari shot him a suspicious look and recognized the
laughter in his eyes. She arched a brow at him and
gave a delicate sniff, something she'd seen Mariette
do on occasion.

"Goodbye, Mrs. Keegan," Mari said, lifting her
chin, tucking her purse under her arm and sailing out
the door. She was so rattled by her brush with Patrick
Keegan that she nearly backed her car into Rose Keegan's mailbox. Then she reminded herself that she was
only pretending to be a woman who lived on the edge,
and she calmed down.

But all the way home Patrick Keegan's handsome
face and mocking eyes stayed in her mind. She figured
that he was in his early thirties, and she hadn't seen a
wedding ring on his hand.

If she were one of those confident, pretty girls with

legs up to their ears, she would have flirted with Patrick Keegan, as irritating as he was. But there was no turning a mouse into a princess. Mari sighed and patted her forehead with the end of her scarf. She had been someone different for all of thirty minutes, and all it had done for her was to make her sweat.

2

"Are you nuts?" Patrick demanded, his blond brows clamping together. He had enough to do this Saturday without having to talk some sense into his grandmother.

"Now, Patrick, is that any way to talk to your grandmother?" Rose asked.

"I don't want you calling that...deranged psychic again. She's a walking disaster area."

"She's a sweet girl."

"She's the most incompetent con artist I've ever seen," Patrick declared.

"She's not a con artist," Rose protested. "Being a police detective has made you cynical."

"Gram, I'm not cynical. I'm realistic. I've arrested more con artists than you can imagine." But none had been quite as bad at deception as Mari. She had been so bad, in fact, that he'd found himself laughing out loud for the longest time after she'd left the previous Sunday.

"Mari's not a con artist," Rose said again. "You can bet on that."

"Mark my words," Patrick said. "You keep calling her and pretty soon she'll be giving you the old song and dance about a curse that needs lifting—for a few hundred bucks.''

''Mari wouldn't do that,'' Rose said indignantly.

''Yes, she would. Which is why I want to be here if you see her again.''

''But, Patrick, you make her nervous.''

''With good reason. Now promise me you won't see her without me around.''

Rose sighed. ''She's coming over this evening.''

''But this is Saturday. I've got a game to coach.'' And he'd promised the boys on the YMCA baseball team that he would get them sodas afterward.

''Then you won't be here, will you?'' Rose asked pointedly.

''I'll be here,'' Patrick told her grimly. ''I wouldn't skip our little Miss Mari's return engagement for anything.''

He had an ulterior motive, but he didn't tell Rose. It wouldn't do for his grandmother to know that Patrick had felt a definite twinge of sexual awareness when he'd stood close to Mari. He had never in his life been attracted to a woman who was less than lawabiding, and he wanted to prove to himself that he was mistaken about that fleeting moment.

Mari glanced at the silver ball on the passenger seat of the car and grimaced. *Dumb idea.* Even genuine psychics didn't use crystal balls anymore, especially crystal balls that weren't really crystal. This one looked like a cannonball that had been painted metallic silver, and it weighed a ton. It belonged to Mari's neighbor, Mrs. Kurtz. It was the late Mr. Kurtz's bowling ball. His widow had had the finger holes filled in before setting the thing in the middle of a flower bed. In desperation, Mari had asked to borrow it today. Mrs. Kurtz had given her an odd look, but she was of stoic Norwegian stock and seldom asked questions.

Mari squared her shoulders as she got out of her car at Rose's house. She really was going to straighten out this misunderstanding today. She couldn't let Rose continue to think of her as a psychic.

She had started to tell her on the phone, but Rose sounded so eager to see her again that she had postponed the confession. Rose had hinted that her grandsons didn't get around to visiting her very often. And then Rose had said she would be mighty interested in seeing Mari's crystal ball. Thus, Mr. Kurtz's bowling ball was pressed into service. But Mari hadn't counted on the thing weighing twenty pounds.

She heaved the ball from the seat and staggered up the walk with it. The door presented a dilemma, because she was afraid that if she set the ball down, it might roll off the small porch and right down the driveway. She made a good attempt at pressing the doorbell with her shoulder but missed. Before she could try again, Rose opened the screen door and ushered her inside.

"My goodness, that's a handful," Rose exclaimed.

"Well, the heavier they are, the more information they pack," Mari said, panting as she maneuvered the ball to the couch and sat next to it.

"Then that one must be a regular encyclopedia," Rose said.

"I spend a lot of time looking at it," Mari said. In truth, she spent every evening staring out her apartment's kitchen window at it as she did her dishes.

"Well, now," Rose said with relish, "you sit right down here and go into a trance or whatever it is you do. And then see if you can tell me something about my grandson Elroy. That boy is about the best pastry chef in the whole state, but he can't seem to find himself a girl."

Mari glanced once at the picture of big, beefy Elroy with his earring and bit her tongue to keep from telling Rose that any girl meeting him for the first time would probably be scared to death.

Hoping to postpone the "trance" part of her visit and deciding she wasn't quite ready to tell Rose that she was a fraudulent psychic, Mari nodded toward the pictures on the table. "Do you have more grandchildren than Patrick and Elroy?" The mere thought of Patrick made her pulse skitter, but she told herself that was only because he was so suspicious of her.

"Oh, my, yes," Rose said, beaming. "There's Reno—he's Elroy's brother. And Sean and Max—they're Patrick's brothers. Now, Elroy and Reno's daddy is Stephen. He's my firstborn. My other boy, Max, is the daddy of Patrick, Sean and Max. He's a widower now." Rose shook her head. "I had all boys. And my boys had boys. They're a wild bunch. That's why I want to get a peek into their future, if I could. Just to satisfy my own worries about how they're doing."

"Don't you see them often?" Mari asked, concerned.

"Fairly often," Rose conceded. "But they don't say much about how things are going. I suppose I'm looking for something to stop me from worrying about them."

If it was reassurance that Rose wanted, then Mari was determined to give it to her. "Oh, I've had good feelings about all of them," she said. "Just last night I had a vision of all of them together and looking very happy."

A familiar husky voice came from the other side of the screen door. "Sometimes I have those visions, usually after a couple of beers."

Mari flushed as the door opened and Patrick strolled inside. She tried hard not to stare at him, but it was tough. Those long, muscular legs drew the female eye as naturally as flowers drew bees. He was wearing jeans again and another T-shirt, this one white. His hair was damp, as though he'd just gotten out of the shower.

"Is your baseball game over already, Patrick?" Rose asked. "Mari was just about to do a reading for me."

"How fascinating," Patrick said dryly. "What is she reading this time? Tea leaves? Ads in the newspaper?"

"I should be going," Mari said stiffly. She started to stand, but Patrick's hand came down firmly on her shoulder, preventing her from rising.

"Stay awhile," he said, a muscle in his jaw tightening. "I'm looking forward to this reading you're going to do. After all, the one you did last weekend was especially revealing." He spoke slowly and deliberately, as if each word contained a message just for her.

Mari was mesmerized by the steely light in his eyes. She had a feeling she couldn't leave, even if he weren't practically holding her to the couch. There was a tingling warmth where his hand rested on her shoulder, and she could feel a trickle of perspiration on the back of her neck.

His hand tightened. Mari felt trapped.

Patrick smiled to himself in satisfaction. He was deliberately intimidating her, and it appeared to be working. He wanted to send a clear message that Mari could take her little con game somewhere else. Nobody got the better of Patrick Keegan's family, certainly not this misguided airhead.

At least she'd had the sense not to wear another of those silly Gypsy outfits this time. Her costume had been overkill, though he had to admit that she'd looked kind of cute.

She shifted away from him. Patrick frowned as her lilac blouse gaped and he caught a glimpse of a small creamy breast cupped in lace. His groin ached suddenly. But even though she had small, sweet breasts, a round fanny and warm brown eyes, he was still going to throw the book at her as soon as she got around to wheedling money from his grandmother.

"I believe you were about to gaze into your crystal ball," he reminded her sharply.

"Yes, well, I'm not sure I'm up to it at the moment," she said, and he caught her eyeing the door hopefully.

Patrick released her and stepped back. He realized that he was no longer interested in simply scaring her away. He was almost looking forward to another of her incompetent but entertaining performances.

"Don't disappoint us," Patrick said, suppressing a smile at the look of incipient panic around her eyes.

She shot him a look of pure malevolence, making

it harder for him to hide his amusement. She had instigated this little farce, and he wanted to watch her try to wiggle her way out of it now that he had her number.

To his surprise, she pursed her lips together and kicked off her shoes. "Do you mind if I put my feet on the couch?" she asked Rose.

"Of course not, dear."

Mari swung her feet up to sit cross-legged, a frown of fierce concentration on her face. She smoothed her white linen pants, then stared down at the silver ball as if she could disintegrate it with her eyes. Bowing her head slightly, she caught Patrick Keegan's distorted reflection in the ball. He was standing slightly behind her, a smirk on his face. Mari's mouth tightened. He was having fun at her expense again. His obvious amusement had her addled enough, but add to it the fact that he practically oozed male sexuality and she was lucky if she could remember her telephone number, much less invent a psychic prediction.

Mari closed her eyes and took a deep breath. She tried to remember everything Rose had said about her family and put it all together with the photos on the table.

"Your grandson—Elroy," Mari began with determination.

"Tell me something, honey," Patrick said casually. "Did you go to school to learn this psychic business?"

Mari gritted her teeth. "Ye-ess," she hissed. She waited a second, then, when he didn't say anything else, she went on. "Your grandson, Elroy—the chef."

"I believe we already established that he's a chef," Patrick said. "Just where did you go to school?"

Mari glared into the silver ball. "Psychic High," she growled out. "I was voted Most Likely To Lead A Normal Life." That had been her actual designation in her own high school yearbook.

He made a choked sound, and Mari waited for some pointed comment. When none was forthcoming, she tried to get back to the business at hand.

"Elroy is very good at...pastry."

"Do you have psychic school reunions, honey?" came the amused male voice behind her. "I don't suppose you'd even have to mail out invitations, would you? Everybody would just know."

Mari had had enough. She uncoiled from the couch and spun around to face him, hands on hips, all five feet four and three-quarter inches of her radiating fury.

"I've already given away too many secrets," she snapped, jutting her chin out at him. "I could get thrown out of the union now, you know."

"Well, we can't have that," he said, shaking his head.

"Now, if you'll excuse me, I'm late for my Saturday evening movie date. We're going to sit home and mentally project it onto the TV screen." She stepped into her shoes and swept out of the house, letting the screen door slam behind her. From inside, she could hear the sound of rich, male laughter. That only made her more irritated, and she jammed the car key into the ignition.

All right. She had brought this all on herself by lying and pretending to be something she wasn't. But Patrick Keegan was the most insufferable male she had ever met. He might be drop-dead gorgeous, but another minute in his company and that bowling ball would have been jammed down his throat. *The bowling ball!* She realized belatedly that she had left it on the couch in her hurry to get out of there. Now what was she going to tell Mrs. Kurtz?

Before she had time to formulate a plan, the screen door opened and Patrick came out, carrying the ball. It irritated her even more to see that he carried it easily.

"I believe you left your window to the future behind," he said dryly as he reached through the passenger side and dropped the ball onto the seat.

"Thank you," Mari said stiffly, nearly groaning when she saw that he had placed it so that the name Brunswick was on top.

"My pleasure," Patrick said. "And, if you're planning on carrying this around with you, you might want to think about getting a bowling bag to put it in. Otherwise, you're going to be giving yourself a hernia. But then, you probably already saw that when you were checking out the future."

Mari ground her teeth again and put the car in reverse.

"You have a nice day now," Patrick said with satisfaction.

Mari backed out of the driveway so fast that Patrick braced himself for the sound of some irritated driver hitting his horn. But she apparently negotiated the street without incident.

He was still smiling as he turned back to the house. She had looked as though she would have loved to strangle him with her bare hands. She was such a little bit of a thing, pretending to read the future and making a mess of it. But she was playing a dangerous game, a game that could get her in big trouble. He didn't like to think of that cute little fanny parked in a jail cell. He had felt that same jolt of sexual awareness again today, but now he was pretty sure it was due to the fact that he was anticipating setting Mari straight as soon as she stepped out of line.

In the meantime, maybe he could enjoy himself a bit. He could string her along while she played psychic for his grandmother, and then, the minute she made an illegal move, he would scare the living daylights out of her. Let her know he was a cop and threaten to let her hang by her pinkies if she didn't reform. Yeah, the threat of fraud and deceptive practices ought to put the fear of the law into her.

"You were very rude to our guest, Patrick," Rose said disapprovingly as he came in the door. "We've probably seen the last of her."

"I think I can guarantee we'll see her again, Gram," Patrick said, picking up the small notepad beside the phone and writing Mari's license number on it. "I'm going to issue a personal invitation."

"Patrick Keegan," Rose said accusingly, "just what are you up to now?"

"Don't worry, Gram," he said, smiling innocently. "I'm going to be very nice to our little fortune teller. You didn't tell her I'm a cop, did you?"

"No, but I'm beginning to think I should have."

"Let's save that surprise for later," Patrick said, his smile as self-satisfied as his grandmother had ever seen it.

Mari was still seething when she lugged the bowling ball back to Mrs. Kurtz's yard just before noon the next day. She settled it on the ground beside the petunias as Mrs. Kurtz came out her back door with a watering can.

"I hope it was useful, dear," Mrs. Kurtz said, a hopeful note in her voice.

"It was perfect for the...party," Mari said. Mrs. Kurtz might be hungry for details, but Mari was too embarrassed by last evening's fiasco to provide them. Mrs. Kurtz wouldn't believe that Mari had tried to palm herself off as a psychic. Not Mari Lamott, staid owner of the Right Note music shop and drab but dependable chairwoman of her church's Sunshine Committee. Mari was the kind of woman who recycled her trash, who baked brownies for shut-ins, who always stayed to help clean up after a church supper, and who played piano at the Sunset Acres Rest Home on Wednesday nights. She was also the kind of woman who longed for just a touch of excitement in her life. And she had felt that when she pretended to be a fortune-telling psychic. There had been sparks in the air when she'd walked into Rose Keegan's home with her crystal ball. Of course, there had been even more sparks when Patrick Keegan arrived.

Mari had thought about him a lot since last night. He had infuriated her by making fun of her psychic reading, but then, she had brought that on herself. If only she were more exotic, more interesting, more...sexy. She had gathered that Patrick Keegan coached a boys' baseball team, so he was athletic as well as handsome. She supposed that women threw themselves at him on a regular basis.

Not that she was planning on throwing herself at Patrick Keegan. She had a feeling it was a catch he would most likely drop like a hot potato. But, it would be nice to be noticed for once. No man had ever been interested in her piano playing or her work at church or even her brownies. But a psychic, now there was an interesting woman.

Surely it wouldn't hurt to continue the charade for just a little longer. After all, Rose Keegan seemed to enjoy her company, and she wasn't really hurting anyone.

Rose's home felt warm and inviting, the kind of home Mari had always wanted. Mari's mother was a single parent, an alcoholic to boot, and Mari had learned at an early age to take on the responsibilities of adulthood. And when her grandmother moved in with them, there were even more responsibilities. Keeping the peace was a never-ending task. She had always wondered how a real home felt.

Mrs. Kurtz made a few more polite comments, but her eyes kept straying over Mari's shoulder, and when Mari turned to go home, she saw why.

Patrick Keegan was standing at the wooden gate dividing the two properties, his forearms leaning casually on top.

"You seem to have a visitor, dear," Mrs. Kurtz called after Mari. It was obvious that she was hoping Mari would make introductions.

"So I do," Mari murmured, her eyes narrowing. Now how did he find out where she lived?

She stopped in front of Patrick and tried to look unimpressed, a difficult feat when her eyes couldn't seem to stop staring at his chest. It was such a nice chest, solid and muscular and pretty impressive under that soft chambray shirt. Of course his legs were pretty impressive, too. His jeans outlined his hard thigh muscles to perfection.

"Why, Miss Lamott," he said in a low, amused voice as she drew near, "I do believe you're checking me out."

Mari blushed to the roots of her hair as she realized that she'd been staring at his thighs.

She was so embarrassed that for a moment it didn't register that he had not only found out where she lived, but he knew her last name, as well.

Patrick took advantage of her discomfiture to do a bit of looking himself. She certainly had sweet little curves, and that soft, bouncy hair gave her a youthful, innocent look that he suspected was in sharp contrast to her devious little mind.

Patrick had run her license number through the computer, and he now knew that her name was Mariel Lamott, she was thirty years old, and she lived above the music store. Discovering that her name was Mariel and not Mariette as she had advertised only reinforced his suspicions about her motives. Most would-be scam artists adopted a name close to their real one. That way, they were less likely to forget who they were supposed to be. And he was pretty sure that little Mariel Lamott couldn't remember her own phone number, much less a fake name too different from her own. She was a scheming little airhead, but he was going to cure her of that. She was going to become the first student of Patrick Keegan's Scared Straight School.

He put on his best innocent smile as Mari recovered from her embarrassment and regarded him suspiciously.

"How did you know where I live?" she demanded.

Patrick started walking toward her apartment, inspecting the small yard as he went.

"I called the police department, gave them your license number and said I'd bumped your car in a parking lot and didn't have any paper with me to leave a note."

"And they gave you my name and address?" she demanded with wide eyes.

"I sound very trustworthy on the phone," he assured her, stopping briefly to admire a small flower bed overflowing with shasta daisies.

"But that's so underhanded," she protested.

"Isn't it, though?" His smile couldn't have been more charming. "I want to talk to you. Aren't you going to invite me in?"

"I don't think so," she said with a frown. "Quite frankly, Patrick, I'm not sure I trust you."

"Really?" He looked disappointed. "Maybe your neighbor would vouch for me."

"Mrs. Kurtz?" Mari looked at him doubtfully. "Do you know her?"

"No, but I can introduce myself."

With an overabundance of confidence in his step, Patrick jogged to the fence and called Mrs. Kurtz's name. She came to attention immediately, having inched closer to the fence with her watering can in what Mari suspected was a subtle attempt to overhear her conversation with Patrick.

"I'm Patrick Keegan," he told her. "My grandmother is Rose Keegan on Spring Street. I would very much like to see Miss Lamott's apartment, but I need someone to vouch for my character. Do you think you could do that?"

Mrs. Kurtz actually blushed as she grinned. Mari didn't remember ever seeing the woman do either before. While Mrs. Kurtz pressed one fluttering hand to her bosom, Patrick pulled out his wallet and showed her his driver's license.

In a matter of moments they had established that his grandmother, Rose, lived two blocks from Mrs. Kurtz's older sister, Leah, who had recently taken a tour of England. It turned out that Patrick's father had once helped neighbors install a TV antenna for her. Mrs. Kurtz was also extremely effusive in her thank-yous to Patrick for something he did for Leah's grandson. Mari couldn't make out what it was, because Patrick had turned Mrs. Kurtz away from Mari while they discussed it.

In the end, Mrs. Kurtz was more than willing to vouch for Patrick, leaving Mari to lead him reluctantly through the back door of the music shop.

"This shop is yours?" Patrick asked in surprise as she continued walking past the rows of guitars and sheet music and the display racks of picks and brightly colored straps.

"Even a psychic needs something to fall back on," she said dryly.

She saw the first genuine smile he'd given her since they'd met. "Do you play an instrument?" he asked.

"Piano and violin," she told him, opening the door to her staircase. That sounded so pedestrian that she impulsively said over her shoulder, "And I've been studying the zither." Now that sounded like something a glamorous fortune teller would play.

In reality, Mari had only seen a couple of zithers in her life—at folk music festivals—and to her they seemed neither glamorous nor terribly interesting. What she did like was the little Irish pennywhistle, actually a small flute, she kept in her purse for odd moments of pleasure. But that was hardly something she would confide to this man whose girlfriends probably played drums or steel guitars or taught aerobics classes.

"The zither, huh?" Patrick said, stopping at the top of the stairs and looking around at the apartment.

"I had to send mine away to be repaired," she said in case he might be thinking of requesting an impromptu concert. "Broken string."

"I see." There was a hint of a smile at his mouth again, but he refrained from comment as he moved to the refrigerator to inspect the magnets there, souvenirs from all parts of the United States plus one from Australia and another from Canada.

"Looks like you enjoy traveling," he said.

"I pick up and go at the drop of a hat," she assured him, crossing her fingers behind her back the way she had as a child. The truth was that she had once brought home one little refrigerator magnet from a church outing to a theme park, and everybody got the idea that she collected them. Now everyone in her church and at the Sunset Acres Rest Home passed along the magnets that their families picked up on vacations.

Patrick wondered silently how many little scams she had pulled in her various travels. If they were as ineptly done as her psychic performance, then it was a wonder she wasn't permanently behind bars. That thought bothered him. He didn't like to think of her under arrest, which was why he was going to straighten her out in a way she'd never forget.

The apartment was neat and spacious, with gleaming hardwood floors and whitewashed walls. The staircase opened into the kitchen, which flowed into a living area. Beyond that was a closed door that he assumed led to the bedroom and bath. He could see a balcony through the French doors in the kitchen. The furniture was comfortable and cheery. Needlepoint pillows rested here and there on the couch and chairs. Patrick thought of the hooker he'd once arrested who took up needlepoint to while away her hours in jail. Cynically, he wondered if Mari had done her pillows in a similar setting.

"Would you like something to drink?" she asked hesitantly, and he noticed that she was backed up almost flat against the refrigerator, as if she expected him to attack her.

"Anything's fine," he said, turning his back to give her some breathing room. In time, he planned to scare her, but right now he wanted her relaxed enough that she would feel safe in continuing her little con game.

He heard her set two glasses on the table and as he turned around, a cat mewed at his feet. It was a dark tabby with a white tip on its tail. Patrick stepped around it and sat down.

"Sorry, Rex," Mari crooned to the cat when he jumped onto her lap. "No salmon today."

Patrick had never trusted women who kept cats. He had a deep, abiding suspicion that it was an outlet for their predatory instincts. And he wasn't about to get within grabbing distance of any woman with predatory instincts, because nine times out of ten, she was the kind of woman who relished the challenge of hooking a man and then wringing him for everything she could get. Not that he mistrusted all women. Just the ones who preferred aerobics classes and malls to their husbands.

He studied the glass of dark red liquid in front of him, then took a tentative taste.

"What *is* this?" he demanded. "I think your wine went flat."

Mari laughed. "That's not wine. It's cherry Kool-Aid."

Patrick just stared at her. He had had many women offer him a drink before, but never had one set Kool-Aid in front of him. Beer, wine, iced tea or soda, but never Kool-Aid.

"You drink this on a regular basis?" he asked warily.

Mari nodded. "I used to keep some beer around—just in case company dropped by—but it never got drunk." She blushed, realizing she'd just admitted that she seldom entertained.

"And you never get an urge to drink anything stronger than this?" he asked, gesturing toward the glass.

Mari shook her head emphatically. "I made the mistake of drinking a bit too much sherry once." She sighed and blushed even more. "I spilled every family secret I'd ever been told. It was very embarrassing."

So, alcohol loosened her tongue. Patrick smiled to himself. He was sure he could use that information at some point in the future.

"You said you wanted to talk to me," she reminded him when he sat watching her without saying a word. She chewed on her lip, sure that he was about to give her a lecture about how much he disapproved of fortune telling. And then, she would probably have to admit to him that she was only pretending to be a psychic. And that would be the end of her exciting double life.

"My grandmother is very fond of you," Patrick said carefully. "She had two sons of her own, and her sons each had sons. So the family's a little short on females."

"Rose is a nice woman," Mari said, still sure that he was about to forbid her to visit his grandmother ever again. "She reminds me of my own grandmother."

Patrick continued to study her without speaking, and Mari grew uncomfortable. Why didn't he just go ahead and say it?

"Today's Gram's birthday, and we're having dinner at her house," he said finally. "She wants me to invite you."

Mari pursed her lips and studied the checkered tablecloth. "But you don't want me to accept. I get it now. You want me to politely but firmly turn down all of your grandmother's invitations from now on. That's it, isn't it?"

Patrick sighed. "That's not it at all." It was hard trying to maintain his train of thought when she kept scrunching up her mouth like that. It was a cute mouth with a little bow on the top lip, and she was forever chewing on it or sucking in the lower lip or drawing her mouth into an *O* as if she were about to be kissed. It was destroying his concentration.

"Well, what is it, then?" she demanded.

"You're good for Gram," he said carefully. "She has arthritis, and she's in pain a lot. But I think your visits have cheered her up. You've taken her mind off her troubles." That much was true. His grandmother had been a lot more cheerful after Mari's little readings.

"You mean you *want* me to visit her?" Mari asked in disbelief.

"I think it could be beneficial to both of you," he said, watching her face. He found himself shifting in his chair as she chewed on her lip again. He had a sudden urge to kiss her, right on that soft, full lip she was chewing. He frowned at that train of thought.

"Beneficial in what way?" she demanded.

"My grandmother likes you," he said. "She's pretty much restricted to her house by arthritis, so her days are a little tedious. And here you are, leading an exciting life, meeting new people all the time." Patrick was embroidering on his line of logic while he watched her face for clues. She seemed to be receptive to his grandmother, so he decided to offer her something to entice her further. "And Gram doesn't have anyone to fuss over anymore. She'd love to bake cookies for you and have you to dinner now and then. I'm sure that with your busy life—doing readings all the time—you don't have a lot of hours left over to cook."

A guilty flush stole over Mari's cheeks, duly noted by Patrick.

"I don't want to take advantage of your grandmother," Mari said hesitantly.

I'll just bet you don't, Patrick thought grimly.

"It would be her pleasure," he said. "That is, if you can spare the time."

Mari felt another flush of guilt. Of course she could spare the time. And visiting Patrick's grandmother would be no chore for her. She liked Rose. But she shouldn't go on letting Patrick and his family believe that she was someone she wasn't.

Still, how eager to see her would Rose be once she found out that Mari wasn't the exotic psychic she claimed to be? There was another problem, as well. Mari was in deep enough with this lie that she wasn't quite sure how to extricate herself. Maybe, if she just went along with the deception for now, she would think of a way out of it.

"I'd love to visit with your grandmother," Mari said, deciding that it wouldn't hurt to pretend to be more exciting than she was for a little while longer.

"Then you'll come to dinner today?"

"If you're sure it's all right."

"Oh, I'm sure," Patrick said, a half smile on his lips.

He could almost hear the click as his trap sprung. The little airheaded psychic had no idea what was really going on. She was about to learn a lesson about the folly of running con games on a detective's family, courtesy of Detective Sergeant Patrick Keegan.

3

Mari had dropped so many pieces of biscuit down the front of her blouse that she was sure she had enough crumbs in her bra to dredge a chicken. And she was beginning to itch.

The problem was her dress. Actually, it was Mariette's dress. After Patrick issued his invitation to Sunday dinner, Mari had insisted on changing clothes before he drove her to his grandmother's house. After all, if she was going to project a more exciting image, she had to look the part. She had hurriedly dressed in Mariette's blue cotton sundress, then rushed out of the bedroom before she could look in the mirror and change her mind. She wasn't entirely comfortable wearing something that showed so much of her shoulders and, well, her cleavage. But she was determined to become a more exciting woman, and this dress was definitely a step toward excitement.

The dress had always been tight on Mariette, but then, Mariette had worn a heavily padded bra. Mari, smaller than her sister by a whole dress size, hadn't thought far enough ahead to borrow one of her sister's bras.

So, here she sat at Rose's supper table, surrounded

by Rose's grandsons, not daring to lean forward because the dress flopped down far enough to show her bra whenever she did.

And because of her ramrod posture, crumbs from the crusty biscuit she was eating continued to drop down her front.

Mari shifted uncomfortably in her chair and looked up to find Patrick watching her from across the table.

"More biscuits?" he asked politely, holding out the basket. Mari recognized that half smile at the corner of his mouth. He was having fun with her again.

"No, thank you," she said, trying to discreetly dislodge some of the crumbs by brushing her napkin over her chest.

"More chicken and dumplings, dear?" Rose called from the head of the table.

"It's delicious," Mari said honestly, "but I'm getting full."

Elroy Keegan, seated on her left, leaned over and spooned another helping of the chicken onto her plate. "A little thing like you needs some more meat on her bones," he insisted.

"Really, I—"

"And some peas," Reno added. He was seated on her right and was as solicitous of her food intake as Elroy was. "And you're almost out of Gram's apple butter. You have to eat your share and Patrick's, as well. He won't touch apple butter ever since he ate a whole jar when he was four and got sick as a dog."

"And be sure to save room for my éclairs," Elroy told her.

Mari looked up helplessly at Patrick, only to find him grinning. His brothers, Sean and Max, were on either side of him, and they began to tease their cousins.

"Elroy, you're stuffing that young lady like you're going to roast her for next Christmas's dinner," Sean said.

"He's just trying to cover up the fact that he's on his fourth helping," Max chimed in. "Gram, did I ever tell you what a good cook you are? These biscuits are straight from heaven."

"Actually, Mari made the biscuits," Rose said, beaming when her grandsons oohed and aahed and praised Mari until she was blushing from her throat to her hair.

Mari glanced at Patrick and found him studying her silently, which made her even more nervous. She had escaped into the kitchen upon their arrival, grateful for the opportunity to help Rose. It wasn't that she wanted to avoid Patrick and his boisterous brothers and cousins, but she had the distinct feeling that Patrick was hiding something from her. She couldn't figure out what he was thinking when he looked at her the way he was doing now, and she found that more than a little unsettling.

"Why don't I clear the dishes?" she suggested, pushing back her chair and beating a hasty retreat to the kitchen.

Patrick leaned back in his chair and grinned. He hadn't missed Mari's discomfort with both the praise and the biscuit crumbs that kept falling down the front of that dress. His brothers and cousins had taken to her immediately, much the way his grandmother had. He had warned them ahead of time that Mari didn't know he was a detective, and he wanted to keep it that way. They didn't understand why, but after some general teasing, they agreed to keep his secret.

He could understand why everyone seemed to find her so appealing. She was cute, and she had that sweet way of chewing on her lip when she was thinking something over. And she had certainly seemed interested in his relatives' various stories during dinner. Once he got her on the straight and narrow path, he imagined that she would be a nice catch for some man. She was the kind of woman who could look downright sexy meandering out of the kitchen in a little sundress with a plate of biscuits in her hands.

Now why the dickens was he entertaining thoughts like that?

Patrick frowned and got up to carry his plate to the kitchen. Rose's hand on his arm momentarily stopped him.

"Now don't go around looking surly like that, Patrick. I think you've already scared Mari."

"Good," he said, his scowl deepening. It was going to take more than biscuits and a cute mouth to make him go easy on Mari Lamott.

He walked into the kitchen to find her leaning over the wastebasket in the corner, performing a hasty shimmy to dislodge the crumbs in her cleavage. She didn't hear him until he cleared his throat, and then she jumped back as if caught pilfering the silverware.

"You startled me," she accused, her face flushing.

"Those biscuits were so flaky they all but melted in the mouth," he said with a glint of amusement in his eyes.

Mari opened her mouth to explain what she had been doing, but she couldn't quite bring herself to tell

Patrick that she had half a biscuit's worth of crumbs lodged in her bra. At the same time she realized that he had just complimented her and teased her at the same time. She started to take a step backward as he moved toward her, then stopped herself. Now that she was the new, exciting Mari Lamott, she was determined not to spend any more of her life backing away from unfamiliar situations. And it was definitely unfamiliar having a good-looking man like Patrick Keegan bearing down on her with a devilish glint in his eyes.

"I'm glad you enjoyed the biscuits," she said hesitantly, her eyes widening as he stopped just in front of her. "I'll just get the rest of the dishes and start rinsing them for Rose."

Patrick sidestepped to prevent her from leaving. He had no intention of letting her hide in the kitchen. "Apparently you're a woman of many talents."

"I am? I mean, yes, I guess I am." She tried to read his expression, wondering just what he was getting at now.

"You have a little apple butter on your nose," he said, and, despite her nervousness, her eyes drifted closed as he reached out a finger to remove it.

Patrick smiled. He knew that she was wondering what he was going to do next, and he couldn't wait for her reaction to his plan. In the meantime he sneaked a peek down the front of that tantalizing sundress, his smile widening when he saw the creamy skin of her breasts, still sprinkled with biscuit crumbs.

"Maybe I should use a washcloth," she suggested hesitantly, and he realized he had been stroking her nose far too long.

He cleared his throat and erased the smile as she opened her eyes. "I think it's all off now," he said. "Come on back to the table for dessert."

He took her arm and firmly guided her toward the dining room, and Mari had little choice but to go. Meanwhile her pulse was still skittering from his touch. Apparently the new, exciting Mari Lamott was a lot more susceptible to a man's touch than the old one had been. Or maybe it was just this man's touch.

Patrick took charge as soon as they were back in the dining room, suggesting that Sean clear the table while Elroy served coffee.

"And before we have dessert," Patrick said, his hand still firmly locked on Mari's arm, "I thought we might all enjoy one of Mari's psychic readings. Perhaps she could do the tarot cards for us."

He smiled benignly down at her while she felt her face heating. The rat! He was deliberately baiting her.

Mari sucked in her breath, then smiled right back at him. "What a shame," she said sweetly. "I don't seem to have my tarot cards with me today. And they're my specialty."

"That is a shame," Patrick said, his face filled with regret. Then he brightened. "But maybe we have some around here. Gram, didn't you have a set of tarot cards?"

Rose wrinkled her forehead. "Well, I think I might have at one time. But I don't know where they are now. I couldn't seem to get the hang of reading them, so I stuck them in a drawer somewhere."

"I think I saw them just the other day," Patrick said, pulling Mari with him as he went into the living room. "Somewhere over here." He pretended to search the coffee table before opening the drawer beneath it. "Well, look here!" He held up a pack of cards in triumph. "This must be my lucky day."

"It certainly must," Mari mumbled in irritation. He seemed determined to aggravate her as much as possible, and she frowned up at him as he handed her the cards.

"Go ahead and make yourself comfortable," he told her, moving her firmly to the couch. "Come on over here, everyone."

Mari sat, wondering what she was going to do now. She didn't know any more about tarot cards than she did about palm reading. And now Patrick's cousins and brothers were gathering expectantly in the living room, lowering themselves to sit cross-legged on the floor in front of the coffee table. Rose made her way carefully to the chair next to the couch and sat, reaching out to pat Mari's hand.

Mari appreciated the support, but she was still at a loss. She took the cards from the box and pretended to study them. She couldn't remember anything that Mariette had said when she had practiced on her. Love? Disaster? Intrigue? She had no idea what card meant what. The only thing to do was wing it.

Patrick stood beside the couch, his hands jammed into the pockets of his charcoal slacks. Mari kept sneaking sideway glances at him. She couldn't remember ever having such a strong physical reaction to a man, especially when he'd only touched her nose and, more to the point, when he'd been aggravating her at the same time.

"Do you want to sing the school song from Psychic

High?'' Patrick suggested helpfully when she continued to stare down at the cards.

''No, I'm ready now,'' she informed him pertly, deliberately not looking at him, because she knew him well enough by now to know that he was smiling.

Well, she would just have to bluff her way through this, Mari told herself. She began to shuffle the cards and then she dealt them out facedown on the coffee table.

''Looks like you're about to play solitaire,'' Patrick observed.

Mari shushed him. ''I'm concentrating here,'' she said, frowning.

''I thought the person seeking advice was supposed to shuffle the cards,'' he said, interrupting again.

Was that right? Mari didn't have a clue. Suddenly she was worried that he might know more about this than he had let on.

''Since nobody has sought advice, I'll just have to do a general reading,'' she said with false bravado.

''Maybe I should be the one seeking advice,'' Patrick offered. ''I mean, this being your specialty and all.''

''Fine,'' she snapped, handing him the pack.

She didn't miss the amusement in his eyes as he picked up the cards on the table, added them to the pack and then shuffled. ''I'll just make myself comfortable,'' he said, handing her the pack and pulling over the hassock to sit opposite her across the coffee table.

''Okay, what's your problem?'' Mari demanded, fixing him with a malevolent stare.

''There are so many,'' he said with mock worry.

"Why don't we narrow it down to my love life and my bank account?"

His male relatives all hooted with laughter, and Mari pursed her lips together. He was being cute again, and she decided it was time to give him a taste of his own medicine.

"We'll take a look at both of those *inadequacies*," she told him, dealing out four cards facedown. "Let's start with your current financial affairs."

Mari flipped over the first card and found herself looking at a group of boys jousting with each other, using long poles that had sprouted leaves. Now what the heck did that mean?

"Hmm," she said, pretending to concentrate.

"I hope I don't have any bounced checks," Patrick said dryly.

Mari was thinking hard and didn't bother to respond to his teasing. She remembered Mrs. Kurtz thanking Patrick for all of his help with her sister's grandson. Despite his gruff exterior, he seemed to have a soft spot for anyone who needed help. And, practiced judge of character that she was, she had a feeling that he was an easy touch for most people—excluding her, of course.

"You're very generous with your money," she said at last, deciding that she had hit the mark by the frown that crossed his face. "And your time, as well," she added. "But sometimes people take advantage of you."

"Hey, Patrick," Max called from behind him. "Can I borrow a twenty?" The others laughed, but it was obvious from Patrick's expression that Mari was on to something.

"Any other startling observations?" he asked.

"Not for the moment," Mari said, feeling a spark of triumph. "Let's look at your financial future." She flipped the next card and found herself staring at a seated figure in a red robe with a crown and sword. At the bottom of the card was the word Justice.

Elroy started to make a comment, but Patrick silenced him with a look.

Mari drew a deep breath. "You are going to get your just deserts," she said solemnly.

"What's that supposed to mean?" Patrick asked, trying not to smile. If anyone was going to get their just deserts, it was Mari Lamott.

"Just what I said," she retorted airily. "Shall we go on to the present state of your love life?"

"Oh, by all means."

Mari turned over the next card and tried hard to hide her smile. The card showed an old man with a staff and lantern. Beneath him, the card read The Hermit.

"I think this speaks for itself," she said, holding up the card to general laughter.

To his credit, Patrick's mouth quirked in a half smile.

As Max and Sean kidded him about his supposedly nonexistent love life, he shrugged helplessly. "What can I say? The psychic knows all the answers."

"It looks like things improve in the future," she said, turning over the final card and revealing something called The Lovers, a naked man and woman she decided to turn over quickly.

But Patrick reached out and snared her hand as she attempted to pick up the card.

"Is that a sure thing?" he asked with obvious amusement.

"Nothing's ever sure," she said, trying not to look at his face. She'd found that she didn't think quite as well as she should when she was caught in those green eyes.

"Maybe I should start introducing you to a few of the girls from the restaurant," Elroy offered, and Patrick gave him a weary look as the others chimed in with offers of blind dates.

"Listen up, you jokers," he said. "I have no interest in any of the predatory females you think you're going to parade in front of me. And, by the way, why don't you take some of your own advice?"

Rose snorted in agreement. "I don't know what's wrong with you boys. A handsome lot like this, and not a one of you married yet. Any girl you bring around is history by the second week. It's like you're allergic to women."

"Not women," Max assured her. "Just wedding rings."

"Although," Elroy said, "I think I could work up some serious interest in someone like Mari." He gave Patrick a smile that was only half-teasing, while Mari blushed pink. "Of course, I guess you'd go all territorial over something like that."

Mari realized that she was holding her breath while she waited for Patrick's response. Why *had* he shown up each time she'd come to see his grandmother? And why had he insisted that she come for supper today? His excuse was that his grandmother liked her and needed the female company, but Mari realized that she was hoping that it was more than that. Her spine tingled as she contemplated the possibility of someone like Patrick Keegan showing a genuine interest in her.

He dashed her incipient hopes with one sentence.

"Mari's a friend of Gram's, and no one is going to screw that up by trying to date her." His eyes dared anyone to contradict him. Mari felt a definite disappointment in the pit of her stomach. She shouldn't have expected any other answer. The only other person of the male species who had taken an interest in her was Mr. Harding, a junior high band teacher, and she suspected that was because he had a fetish for knees. Two years ago he had come to the shop one day when she was wearing shorts and had immediately asked her out. On each subsequent date, he had suggested that she wear shorts. When things eventually progressed to the bedroom, he had spent an inordinate amount of time fondling and licking her kneecaps. Their one sexual encounter was a disaster. It lasted all of thirty seconds, and left Mari of the opinion that sex was highly overrated.

"I might have something to say about that," Mari retorted.

Patrick fixed her with an impatient glare. "No, you don't. If anyone wants to ask you out, they're going to have to come through me first." Before she could argue, he jumped to his feet and pulled a small pager from his chest pocket. "Come on. I have to take you home."

"But she hasn't had dessert yet," Elroy protested.

"Pack her a doggie bag," Patrick said, picking up the tarot cards and shoving them back into the box. "I have to go to work."

"You're working on Sunday?" Mari asked in confusion. "I thought you coached a baseball team."

There was a lot of throat clearing and shifting of eyes on the part of everyone but Patrick, whose scowl deepened.

"I do," he said, "and we have a game. Let's go."

Five minutes later Mari was seated in Patrick's car, a bag of éclairs on her lap. She hadn't been rushed out a door so fast since she was five and come into the house after a close encounter with a skunk.

"This coaching job," she said tentatively. "Are you with the high school?"

"Why?" he demanded suspiciously. "Do you know some teachers there?"

Mari was taken aback. "Just the band teachers there and at the junior high."

"I work at the YMCA," he said, watching her face.

"Oh, that sounds interesting. What do you do besides coaching?"

"Lifeguard and run the sports activities," he said, fabricating this job out of thin air. He was glad for the undercover experience he'd had on the police force, because lying had become a practiced art for him.

Mari lapsed into silence when he didn't elaborate, then frowned when he turned the car.

"This isn't the way to my place."

"I know. I have to stop off at my apartment on the way to get my...gym clothes."

"Oh."

They pulled up to his apartment building, and Mari noticed a slinky blonde in pink shorts sitting on the stairs, filing her nails. She sat on the bottom step, long legs stretched out in front of her, her high-heeled sandals emphasizing her slim calves and ankles. Mari sighed. Now there was a pair of knees that the band teacher would have loved.

"Wait here," Patrick warned her unnecessarily. Mari had no intention of following him into his apartment.

The blonde brightened considerably when Patrick drew near, and he stopped momentarily to exchange a few words. From what Mari could overhear—hamburgers, beer, grill—she gathered that the apartment complex in general, or maybe the blonde specifically, was planning a barbecue. Patrick must have declined the invitation, because the blonde looked crestfallen as he continued up the stairs.

The car was only about fifteen feet from the steps, and the blonde kept casting curious glances Mari's way. Finally she called, "You don't have any cuticle clippers in your purse, do you?"

Mari glanced around to see if there were any other potential cuticle clipper suppliers nearby and didn't see a soul.

"No," she said, giving an apologetic shrug.

"I'm thinking of getting some plastic nails put on," the blonde said, ambling over to the car. "What do you think?"

"I hear they can cause a fungus," Mari said, then immediately regretted the words. She was supposed to be the new, exciting Mari, the one who didn't worry about mundane things like fungus.

"I don't know," the blonde said. "I'd kind of like to put some of those designs on them, or maybe glue a little rhinestone on each nail."

"Sounds nice," Mari said noncommittally.

"You on a date with Patrick?" she asked, still sounding unconcerned but watching Mari from the corner of her eyes as she inspected her nails.

"Oh, heavens, no," Mari said. "I was visiting his grandmother, and he's driving me home."

"Oh." The blonde brightened. "I'm Stacey." She extended her hand and shook Mari's. "I asked him to the barbecue next weekend, but he said he was busy. Doesn't he have the most fantastic hands?"

"Nice to meet you. My name's Mari." She didn't know what to say about Patrick's hands, so she let that pass.

Normally, Mari was the poster girl for straightforwardness and honesty, but suddenly she saw a way to pay Patrick back for his incessant aggravation.

"Well, you know how Patrick is," Mari said casually. "The more he sends a busy signal, the more interested he is."

"Really?" Stacey sounded skeptical.

"Oh, sure. His whole family is like that. If you want my advice, I'd keep inviting him to things and maybe show up at his apartment with a jar of apple butter. It's his favorite, you know. And the woman who cooks her own really has the inside track with him."

"You think that might work?"

"I'm sure of it. Just don't get discouraged when he pretends not to be interested."

"Well, it might be worth a try," Stacey said thoughtfully. "Homemade apple butter, you say."

Mari nodded enthusiastically as Patrick came down the steps. He frowned when he saw Mari in conversation with Stacey, and he picked up his pace.

"Sorry we have to run," he called breezily to Stacey as he tossed a gym bag into the back seat. "Mari's late for her knitting class."

"Knitting class?" Mari asked dryly as they pulled away.

"Should I have told her you're a psychic?" he countered. "She'd just love to have a reading."

Mari shook her head, feeling a momentary twinge of guilt for what she'd done to Patrick and Stacey, but it passed when she made herself remember the tarot card reading.

"What did you two talk about?" he asked casually.

"Oh, nothing much." She busied herself refolding the top of the bag of éclairs.

Patrick was looking at her suspiciously. She had always been a bad liar. In fact, she was nearly as bad at lying as she was at giving psychic readings.

"She didn't talk about my work, did she?"

Mari looked at him curiously. "No, why should she?" She frowned. "You're hiding something about your job, aren't you?"

"What's to hide?" he asked. "I work at the Y, and I coach baseball."

But Mari had caught the sudden tightening of his jaw. And he wouldn't quite meet her eyes.

"You *are* hiding something," she accused. "What is it? Do you have to clean the pool there? Or maybe you're in charge of jockstrap procurement. It's something embarrassing, isn't it?"

Patrick rolled his eyes.

Mari snapped her fingers. "I know! You're a masseur there, aren't you? I should have known. That's why Stacey said you have such great hands. That's it, isn't it?"

Patrick tried not to smile. He seriously doubted that anybody actually gave massages at the local YMCA, but if she wanted to believe that he did, it might keep her from finding out what he really did.

"All right," he said, frowning at her. "I'm the masseur. Now promise me you won't say a word to anyone. I get hassled enough as it is."

"It's nothing to be ashamed of," she told him earnestly. "It's an honest living. I mean, if you don't do anything more than give actual massages." Her voice trailed off, and that blush climbed her face again.

Patrick didn't know how the little con artist could still summon up a blush, but Mari managed it. He pulled the car to the curb in front of her shop and turned to face her, his hand on the seat behind her neck. He could smell a soft lavender scent on her hair.

"Now remember," he told her, "I don't like to go around advertising what I do for a living, so I'd appreciate it if you'd just pretend you never heard that."

Mari's eyes sparkled. "On one condition," she said.

"What's that?"

"That you give me a massage some day. I've always wanted one, but I never had the nerve to make an appointment." There was that blush again.

Patrick worked to hide his smile. "All right," he said. "It's a deal." He walked around the car and helped her out. "Remember," he said, reaching out to touch her lips with his finger, "not a word to anyone about my job—or the YMCA, either, for that matter."

Mari nodded, swallowing hard as his finger brushed back and forth lightly a couple of times. She felt a tingling start in her mouth and travel to every curve and crevice of her body. Patrick slowly lowered his finger until it was under her chin. He tilted her head up slightly as she stared at him with wide eyes. He was frowning slightly as his head lowered, and for a moment she thought that he wasn't going to do it after all.

But he did. His mouth touched hers, and the tingling in Mari's body became full-blown electricity. Her lips parted on a sigh, and her hands clutched his shirtfront. She had never been kissed like this before. Mr. Harding had kissed her as if she were a trumpet and he was trying to wring a Sousa march from it. Patrick Keegan's kiss was pure sensuality.

Patrick pulled away abruptly, leaving her trying to kiss the air. Embarrassed, she opened her eyes to find him looking at her with a mixture of irritation and confusion.

"I...thank you for supper," she said, twisting her hands.

Patrick reached down suddenly and plucked up the bag of éclairs she'd dropped on her shoes. "Don't forget dessert."

And then he was stalking back to the car while Mari stared after him in a daze.

He berated himself the entire drive to the station house. Why the hell had he done that? And how could a woman look so innocent and sweet, then kiss like a red-hot siren? He was still smoldering inside from the heat of that kiss.

Mari Lamott was nothing but trouble from her lavender-scented hair to her deceitful little heart.

4

On Friday nights Mari played the pennywhistle. It was one of the pleasures that she rationed out to herself, like the one chocolate bar she let herself have on Sunday evenings.

She would sit on the floor of the small balcony that jutted off her second-floor apartment, her feet curled under her, and focus all of her attention on the small flute.

Mari had recently mastered an old folk tune called "Nell Murphy's Cow," a song about a woman who prized her livestock above her husband. It was a sentiment that Mari could understand considering the aggravation that Patrick Keegan had caused her.

This particular Friday night was the one following the Sunday when Patrick had taken her to supper at his grandmother's house, then unexpectedly kissed her when he brought her home.

Mari hadn't heard a word from him since, which had given her considerable time to study the implications of the kiss. She had come to the conclusion that the new, more exciting Mari Lamott might indeed inspire some man to kiss her, but in Patrick Keegan's case the kiss had probably been unintentional and meant nothing. He was a wordly bachelor—a masseur at the YMCA must meet all kinds of women—and no doubt he kissed females all the time. To him, it was no more than a hello or goodbye.

That explanation didn't do much for her ego, but she hadn't come up with a more reasonable one all week, so she concentrated on "Nell Murphy's Cow" and toyed with the idea of maybe getting herself a potbellied pig to keep her cat company.

After a day of restringing violins at the shop and giving piano lessons to children who no doubt wouldn't remember the experience with pleasure, she had changed into a pink T-shirt and jeans. The evening was warm, tempered by a light breeze.

So immersed in the tin whistle that she didn't hear footsteps, Mari caught a movement in the corner of her eye and looked up to find Patrick Keegan standing on her balcony. She clapped her hand to her chest in lieu of screaming.

"How did you get up here?" she demanded.

"I climbed the stairs." He gestured toward the stairs, and Mari gaped.

"Those rickety things? You're lucky you didn't fall off and kill yourself."

"I decided to live dangerously." He nodded toward the pennywhistle. "That sounded nice. Is it your zither?"

"My zither's still out for repairs," she said. "This is a pennywhistle."

"It doesn't sound like a whistle."

"It's really a little flute." She stared at him self-consciously. "What are you doing here?"

"I had to escape my apartment. For some reason

Stacey keeps showing up at my door with jars of apple butter. You wouldn't know anything about that now, would you?''

Mari blushed. ''Me?''

''Yes, you.'' He folded his arms and looked at her sternly. Since she was still sitting on the floor and she was so little to begin with, he had no doubt that she was intimidated.

But, to his surprise, she gave him a saucy smile.

''You're lucky I haven't gone around telling everyone I know that you're a masseur. I have some elderly friends who would *really* appreciate your talents.'' There were devilish lights in her eyes that nearly made him smile. But he pretended to be cranky instead. He admired her spunk for pulling that little apple butter trick on him, but he couldn't let her get away with it.

''We prefer the term massage therapist,'' he said with a straight face.

''You know,'' Mari told him, climbing to her feet, ''you need to loosen up a little.''

Now it was his turn to be surprised. ''Me? Loosen up?''

She nodded earnestly. ''You take everything far too seriously.''

Patrick regarded her thoughtfully. She had a point, but it was his business to take things seriously. And, even if he had succumbed to the cop's occupational hazard of cynicism, he still had to admit that Mari had provided more levity in his life in the past two weeks than he'd ever had from a woman.

''And what do you recommend for this serious streak of mine?'' he asked.

''You need an evening out.'' She couldn't believe

she was so bold. Maybe this new exciting side of herself was a permanent change.

Patrick didn't say anything for a moment. He had come over here to check up on her after he'd received a report two days ago of a Mariette Lamott who had bounced some checks in the next county on Monday. Apparently the little con artist had been a busy lady this week, because another report came across his desk on Wednesday of this same Mariette Lamott skipping out on a court date for numerous traffic tickets.

When he got off work on Wednesday, he had parked down the street from Mari's shop, planning to keep an eye on her. She had gotten into her car, and he had felt the familiar adrenaline of a chase tempered by a disappointment that she was about to get herself into trouble again. He had followed her to the Sunset Acres Rest Home and watched as she carried a sheaf of papers inside. He couldn't see what they were, but he had his suspicions. He didn't like to think that she was running more con games on senior citizens, but that seemed to be her modus operandi. He was going to have to speed up his program to reform her before he had no choice but to lock her up.

"An evening out," he repeated. This was just what he was planning. "What do you have in mind?"

"Some dinner and maybe a little dancing?"

She sounded unsure of herself, but he decided that that was only natural given her propensity for trouble. Her brain was probably scrambling to figure out what she could get out of him.

"All right," he said. "As long as you don't have champagne tastes."

"Oh, this is my treat," she insisted.

"Then I put myself in your hands for the evening," he told her, nearly smiling when she blushed for him, because he knew that the mention of hands had started her thinking about massages again.

Well, Mari thought as she gathered her purse and keys, she had actually asked Patrick Keegan out on a date! And she had insisted on paying for it herself. She truly must be an exciting, modern woman to pull off something like that. She was liking this new side of herself more and more.

Patrick was standing on the balcony with his back to her when she returned, and she took a moment to admire the way he looked. A light breeze ruffled his thick, blond hair, and as he leaned his arms on the railing she could see hard, corded muscles in every place where his light blue golf shirt clung. His dark jeans cupped a trim behind and outlined nicely muscled thighs and calves. Mari sighed, and Patrick turned around with a smile.

"Ready?"

"Oh, yes." She recollected herself and cleared her throat. "Would you mind driving? My muffler broke yesterday, and I haven't gotten to the garage yet. I don't want to...well, you know."

"Get stopped by the police?" he proposed helpfully.

She nodded.

Patrick was pretty sure that her aversion to being stopped by the police had more to do with the bounced checks and traffic charges than with a faulty muffler. But he forced a smile onto his face and escorted her down to his car.

Mari directed him to a local pizza parlor where he

unobtrusively looked around as the waitress was seating them, just to make sure he wasn't going to run into anyone who knew him. There were no familiar faces, and he leaned back in the booth after the waitress had taken their orders, a beer for him and an iced tea for Mari.

"So," Patrick said, "tell me about yourself."

"Why?"

No woman had ever been so bluntly uninterested in talking about herself around him before, and it startled him.

"Because that's normal behavior when a man and woman go out to dinner together," he told her.

"I wouldn't know about that," she said, toying with her napkin.

"You wouldn't know about that because..." he prompted.

Mari sighed. He seemed determined to make her admit to her lack of experience with men. But she wanted to pretend that she was far different from the Mari Lamott who hadn't had a date in so long that her social calendar had rusted.

"Because when you're a psychic, it's difficult to develop relationships," she said. "I mean, what would you think if we were in a movie and I suddenly turned to you and said, 'By the way, I don't think you should take that car trip you were planning'?"

Patrick laughed. "I'd think you were joking."

"Don't you believe that sometimes we get a little glimpse into the future?"

Patrick shook his head. "Nope. What happens is what happens. Nothing's decided beforehand."

Mari sat back and chewed her lip. "So you probably

don't believe in destiny where love is concerned, either, do you?''

Patrick actually snorted at that one. "I think that's a load of hogwash," he said. "You show me two people on this planet who are supposedly meant for each other, and I'll show you two people who would most likely be better off alone."

Mari narrowed her eyes. "Is there anything at all that you *do* believe in?"

A slow grin spread over Patrick's face. "Sure. I believe in sleeping in when it's raining, crossing the street with the light and classic rock and roll."

Mari groaned. "You're going to hate where we're going after the pizza."

"Why?"

"You'll see."

He saw what she meant as soon as they entered the big, open lounge that adjoined a bowling alley. But he didn't hate it. On the contrary, it made him smile. Country-western music poured out, and men and women in jeans and flouncy skirts square-danced as a man called out the moves. He wouldn't have guessed that Mari liked square dancing, and the excited light in her eyes made his smile grow.

He noticed that this was an older crowd, and they obviously knew Mari. As the dance ended, several people called her by name and took time to chat with her. After the sixth older gentleman had come over, introduced himself and shaken Patrick's hand, he realized in amusement that they were checking him out to see if he was suitable for Mari.

"She *never* brings a guest," one man confided as

he thumped Patrick on the back. "We'd just about given up on her. My Ethel here—" he looped his arm around a Dale Evans look-alike "—has been trying to get her together with our nephew, Johnny, but you know young folks today. Won't listen to anybody over sixty." He grinned and pressed Patrick's hand again while Mari blushed beside him.

"Let's dance," she suggested as the man and his wife moved away. She was obviously embarrassed, and Patrick pretended not to understand.

"Right now? Why, half the people in this place are lining up to shake my hand, and I'm looking forward to meeting more of your adoring public."

She socked him on the arm, and Patrick laughed as he led her to the sets of couples squaring up on the floor.

He hadn't had such a good time in years, he thought as he drove her home. For some reason he had no trouble relaxing around Mari, though, for the life of him, he couldn't imagine why. He spent half his time with her wondering what kind of trouble she was going to find next.

"Do you want coffee…or something?" she asked hesitantly as he helped her out of the car in front of her apartment.

He definitely wanted something, but it wouldn't do to get himself physically involved with her, not when he was working his brain cells to death trying to find the best way to reform her. A man running on hormones was a loose cannon.

"You do mean real coffee, don't you?" he asked worriedly. "Not coffee-flavored Kool-Aid?"

"Real coffee," she assured him.

As she unlocked the front door to the music shop, he saw that there was no burglar alarm. He almost started citing statistics about break-ins, but he stopped himself. He wasn't going to go nuts worrying about some potential burglar when Mari was running her own illegal activities.

The shop was dark, and Patrick bumped into her as she led the way to the stairs.

"Sorry," he murmured, but he kept his hand at her back.

Mari nearly shivered under the pleasurable sensations emanating from his touch.

Her cat was pacing and meowing when she turned on the kitchen light at the top of the stairs.

"Is your supper dish empty, Rex?" she asked in a soothing voice, bending to pet the cat. Patrick watched as she poured kitty biscuits into the bowl on the floor.

"You do know that Rex is a cat and not a dog?"

"He's really T. Rex, like the dinosaur. And he has a voracious appetite. He's also a chronic worrier. Whenever I leave, he thinks I'll never come home again."

Given her bounced checks and traffic tickets, Patrick thought the cat might have a point.

Mari started the coffee, then put sugar and cream on the table. She arranged some brownies on a plate and carried them to the table, as well, gesturing for him to sit. She wasn't at all accustomed to entertaining a man in her apartment, especially late on a Friday night, and she wasn't sure what else she should do. Put on music? Dim the lights? But those were moves designed to lead to romantic overtures, and she didn't think that Patrick had romance on his mind. And, though she might, she didn't know how to proceed.

Patrick ate one of the brownies, then complimented her on it. "They don't have any special ingredients, do they?" he asked with a raise of his brows, thinking of the two parties he'd busted where marijuana brownies were the main event.

Mari didn't have a clue as to what he meant. "Well, I do use real vanilla," she said slowly, her brow furrowed. "I think it makes a big difference."

"I'm sure it does," he told her, trying not to smile.

When she brought the coffee to the table, Patrick watched her spoon about half the sugar bowl into her cup.

"Honey," he said, "between the coffee, the chocolate and all that sugar, I figure I'm going to have to peel you off the ceiling in about forty minutes. I don't think I've ever known a woman to take so many stimulants at one time."

"Really?" Mari looked at him in interest. "What do the women you know do?"

"What do you mean?"

"Well, for instance, what do they eat?" If she was going to refine her image as the new, exciting Mari Lamott, she might as well get details on female behavior from an expert.

Patrick shrugged. "Well, most of them are on a diet, so they eat salads a lot. Of course, in the evenings they drink beer or wine. Point of fact, you are the only woman who has ever set Kool-Aid or brownies in front of me."

"Oh, dear." She looked crestfallen.

"Not that I'm objecting," he hastened to tell her.

"Well, I can't say I'm crazy about that Kool-Aid, but these brownies are even better than Gram's—and don't tell her I said that."

Mari chewed her lip. She was making mental notes on everything he said. No Kool-Aid. And stock up on beer and wine.

"What do they do in the evenings? On dates, I mean."

"Pretty much what we did," Patrick told her. "Maybe go to the movies. And make out, of course."

"Of course," Mari said. Then she asked shyly, "How do they make out?"

"You mean you want details?"

"Well, yes, if you don't mind."

"Honey, did you grow up in a convent?"

Mari blushed. "Not exactly. But I was sheltered...and shy." In fact, Mari was too busy monitoring her mother's drinking, helping her grandmother with the housework, and trying to keep Mariette out of trouble, to do any dating while she was growing up. She was bookish and immersed in her music anyway, and by college she had turned shyness into an art form. She was so paralyzed by fear of making a fool of herself that her only experience with the male sex was with Mr. Harding, and even though she wasn't technically a virgin any longer, she wasn't sure if that thirty seconds counted as real sex or not.

"So you never necked with a guy before?" Patrick asked in disbelief.

"Of course I did," she said, too embarrassed to admit that the band teacher had been her only experience. "But he wasn't from around here, and I don't think he did it right."

"What was he, an alien?" Patrick asked dryly.

"He was allergic to perfumes and soaps," Mari said defensively. "So he couldn't do much touching." Other than her knees.

Patrick sighed. Either she was giving him one big line of bull or else she really had been sheltered. "Come here," he said, standing and heading for the couch. He sat and then patted the seat next to him. Mari sat, feeling a little foolish but mostly excited.

Patrick studied her face for a moment. She looked totally guileless and innocent, but he was cynical enough to believe she was neither of those things. He was pretty sure that she was trying to do a number on him, get him so ensnared in her charms that he wouldn't notice when she tried to get money from his grandmother. But, despite his scruples, he was intrigued enough by her gambit to go along, for a while anyway.

He reached out to feather his finger down her cheek and felt her go totally still beneath his touch. His wandering finger traced her lips. He could feel her breath quicken.

"I'll stop anytime you tell me to stop," he told her, but she just gazed back at him, wide-eyed.

Patrick took hold of her shoulders and turned her until her back was to him, then pressed her down on his lap so that she was looking up at him. She felt stiff as a board, and he gently brushed back her hair.

"Just relax," he told her. "This isn't like a visit to the dentist, you know."

"It isn't? I mean, I know it isn't." She had made a visible effort to relax, but she was still one straight line from her neck right down her back to her legs and toes.

She was either a consummate actress, or she really didn't have any experience with men. Patrick decided to take things easy just in case she was actually frightened. He feathered his hand down her neck, barely touching her with the pads of his fingers. Pausing only briefly, he trailed his hand lower, skimming her breasts and stomach. She shivered violently, and Patrick murmured, "Easy, honey. I'm not going too fast for you, am I?"

"No," she whispered, her voice barely audible.

"Now we're just going to loosen things up here a bit," he told her as he slowly undid the button of her jeans, then lowered the zipper.

"Shouldn't I be doing something?" she murmured worriedly. "I mean, I've always heard that men don't like passive women."

"You don't have to do anything, honey," he said, trying not to smile. "We'll take it nice and slow."

He lifted the T-shirt next, and when his finger did a soft exploration of one breast, Mari arched to his hand, a soft moan escaping her mouth.

Patrick reached under her and expertly undid her bra clasp. He pushed it up and looked down at her small, ivory breasts with peach-colored nipples. He felt himself growing aroused, and he shifted her slightly. His hand went back to her breast, softly stroking in circles, moving closer to the nipple without touching it. She continued to arch to his touch, and her hands gripped the couch cushion.

Patrick reached behind her to lift her slightly. He crossed one leg, then lowered her back. Now she was in comfortable kissing distance, and he discovered that he was looking forward to this next step in their necking session.

He began at her neck, nipping lightly, then kissing her until she was squirming. He moved lower slowly, tasting her sweet skin, letting his tongue explore each little hollow and peak. When he started on her nipples with his mouth, she jerked and moaned.

"Patrick, I want to...I can't stay still," she gasped, reaching up to clutch his back. Her fingers pressed tightly as he laved her breast again. She was squirming continuously now, soft, sweet sounds issuing from her throat. Patrick knew that he should stop, but she was so responsive that he couldn't resist sliding one hand down the front of her open jeans and gently exploring there, as well.

He raised his head to nibble on her neck again, but she arched up and began kissing him instead. His tongue tasted her lips, then found its way inside her mouth. She touched it tentatively with her own tongue, her kisses full of hunger.

Patrick's groin hardened even more, and he found himself breathing hard. His hand began to peel down her jeans before he even realized what he was doing. He raised his head fractionally and caught sight of her liquid brown eyes glazed with passion.

Suddenly he realized how far gone he was. One more minute of kissing her like this and he would be stripping her of her panties. Despite the fact that she had all but initiated this, he felt as if he was taking advantage of her.

Mari whimpered and tried to pull him back to her.

"Easy, honey," he whispered raggedly. "I think we've gone far enough for tonight."

He began to gently restore her clothes, and when he glanced at her face he saw that she was blushing again.

"I'm sorry," she murmured, sitting up. "I guess I'm not too good at this."

"You're just fine," he assured her. Seeing how crestfallen she looked, he added, "I don't have any protection with me, and I don't want to take a chance."

"Protection?" she asked in confusion.

"Condoms," he clarified.

Her face flushed even more. "Oh." She was obviously a failure as a modern woman. First, no beer and now no condoms. She was going to have to stock up on the essentials if she was going to pass muster as the new and exciting Mari Lamott.

"Don't worry," he said, helping her off his lap and brushing back her hair. "Necking takes a little practice."

Mari brightened at this. "Can we do it again?"

"Not right now," he said gently, thinking that if he indulged in any more necking with her at the moment he was going to rip his jeans. "We have plenty of time." Plenty of time provided he got her to stop her dangerous con games before she got herself into more hot water. He was going to have to work harder on her rehabilitation. The way she looked at him with those big brown eyes was clouding his judgment. And her skin had the sweetest smell.

"I'll come over tomorrow," he said, heading for the stairs.

Mari brightened as she followed him downstairs. "Are we going to neck again?"

"Not first thing, honey," he said. "I'm going to replace the muffler on your car." He paused at the foot of the stairs, trying to see her face in the dark music shop. "You really do need a new muffler, don't you?"

"Of course I do," she said, confused. "But, I don't understand. Why are you going to replace it for me?"

"Because men and women do little things like that for each other. Especially when they've started necking."

"What should I do for you?"

"Well..." Patrick considered his many options. He could ask her to stop doing her psychic readings. But that was too easy. And he liked the thrill of the chase. He wanted to reform her in a more dramatic way. And besides, he was enjoying this cat and mouse game they were playing. "How about if you fix me lunch?"

"All right. Any preferences?"

"A sandwich would be great." He leaned over and kissed her gently on the nose. "See you tomorrow."

Mari nearly floated up the stairs after she let him out.

"You know, Rex," she said to the cat who sat cleaning his paws on the counter, "I can feel myself changing every day. You know what I might just do? I might just order myself something from one of those Victoria's Secret catalogs."

Rex looked up and blinked at her momentarily, then went back to his grooming.

5

Mari got her bicycle from under the stairwell in the music shop late the next morning. It would be more convenient to use her car, but she didn't know what time Patrick would arrive. And she definitely didn't want him to take the new muffler and go home if he found her car gone.

Just to be safe, she wrote a brief message on a Post-it note, telling him she would be right back, and stuck it to her windshield.

Party! Party! Party! was a twenty-four-hour shop five blocks away. Mari had never been inside it before, but she figured this was a good time to start. She needed to acquire the trappings of a modern, exciting woman.

A young man with acne, who looked barely old enough to have graduated high school, much less sell liquor, manned the lone cash register. Mari would have preferred a female clerk, for advice if nothing else, but she had decided she could deal with this.

She cruised the aisles, staring at the rows of alcohol and wishing she knew what she was doing. Her mother had drunk whiskey, and Mari had deliberately avoided learning anything about alcohol given her mother's erratic behavior.

The only solution to her ignorance seemed to be to buy one of everything. She couldn't afford that, so she did the next best thing, chose the cheapest bottle from each aisle. She began lining up her purchases next to the register while the boy clerk watched with growing interest.

She stopped at ten bottles and a six-pack of beer. She frowned as she surveyed her cache—vodka, Scotch, rum, gin, whiskey, wine, and four bottles of liqueurs. She'd been particularly intrigued by the chocolate schnapps. She made a final sweep of the store, stopping at the rack of men's magazines. Neatly displayed on a nearby shelf was an impressive array of condoms. Now she faced the same dilemma as she had with the liquor—such a wealth of choices that she didn't know what to pick. She decided on the same solution, a sampling of everything.

When she dumped her newfound riches on the counter, the clerk gawked. He stared at Mari a moment before he began ringing up the three men's magazines and the five boxes of condoms, one plain, one ribbed, one with lubricant, one that glowed in the dark and one strawberry-flavored.

"You have a good day, ma'am," he said to Mari, his voice cracking as he handed her her change. Mari had to make two trips to her bike with the bags, and it took a great deal of rearranging, but she finally got everything but the beer packed into the large basket that hung over the bike's rear wheel. She draped the six-pack over the front handlebars and began a wobbly trip home.

"Ma'am?" the boy called from the door, obviously anxious about asking this particular question. "You aren't having a rave party, are you? I've never been to one of those."

Mari had no idea what a rave party was, but she was pretty sure she wasn't having one.

"Sorry," she said. "Just stocking up."

"Jeez," the clerk said in disappointment as she pedaled away.

By the time Mari reached her own shop, she was winded and her legs hurt. But she perked up as soon as she saw Patrick's car parked behind her own in the small alley that ran next to her shop. He was dressed in old jeans and a once-white T-shirt, and he had a box of tools on the ground near her car.

He looked up as she pedaled laboriously to a stop. His eyes went first to the six-pack on the handlebars and then to the necks of the liquor bottles sticking out of her rear basket.

"You having a big party?" he asked, picking up one of the bags, then the other.

Mari shook her head. "Just stocking up."

His brows went up as he followed her through the shop, but he said nothing. Then, when he set the bags down on her kitchen counter and took a quick peek inside, his brows went up even farther.

"Stocking your library, as well?" he asked, holding up the three magazines she'd purchased "*Babes With Big Buns*, *Love Knots*, and *Male to Male*."

Mari blushed and snatched away the bag before he could get to the condoms. "I'm doing research," she said. "I thought I should find out what men like."

"If you'd looked through this before you bought

it," he said, pushing *Male to Male* toward her, "you'd have noticed that what these men like is other men."

"Oh?" She furrowed her brow, not understanding what he meant. Then she opened the magazine to the center. "Oh!"

"You may notice that the men who read these other magazines have...specialized interests, as well."

She wasn't about to check that out at the moment, not with him standing right there with that half smile on his face. "Would you like something to drink?" she asked to change the subject.

"Maybe later," Patrick said, eyeing her cache of liquor skeptically. "I'd better get started on that muffler." He couldn't keep himself from looking over his shoulder as he reached the stairs. Sure enough, she had edged open *Love Knots*. Her eyes widened, and another blush climbed her face.

Patrick chuckled to himself as he went down the stairs.

By noon the muffler was installed and Patrick was more than a little tired. He and his partner had pulled the night shift all week except for yesterday, which had been his day off. And he hadn't slept worth a damn since last night's encounter with Mari.

He had gotten up early this morning to take his grandmother grocery shopping before coming to Mari's. He had helped her shop, unloaded her groceries and listened to a lecture on how much she liked Mari. He refrained from telling her about Mari's little check bouncing and traffic ticket troubles. Once he got Mari straightened out, there was no need for anyone else to find out about her not-so-sterling record. For now, he was looking forward to a long nap.

Patrick was wiping his hands on a rag when Mari came out of the shop. She had on a pair of white shorts and a pink top that made her look feminine and kind of sexy. He frowned when he saw the large, empty coffee can in her hand.

"How much do I owe you for the muffler?" she asked.

Patrick shook his head. "Nothing."

"I can't accept a gift like that," she protested, chewing her lip.

Patrick smiled. "Yeah, a muffler's pretty personal."

"You know what I mean. It must have cost quite a bit."

"Tell you what. You can buy me dinner sometime."

"All right," she said hesitantly. "I left a sandwich on the counter for you. I have to go...do some errands."

"Anything I can help you with?" he asked casually.

"Oh, not really. I can take care of it." She was hesitant to tell him where she was going, because it wasn't the kind of thing she suspected that an exciting woman with an active social life would be doing on a Saturday.

"I have the afternoon free," he insisted, and she noticed that he was watching her intently.

"Well," Mari said hesitantly, chewing on her lip. "Actually, I was going to go collect for the library fund drive. The money has to be turned in Monday, and I haven't had a chance to make the rounds yet."

She shifted her weight, wondering why he suddenly looked so alarmed.

"Money?"

Mari nodded. "I think I can raise quite a bit this afternoon. There are several older people in the neighborhood, and of course they can't give as much because of fixed incomes and all but…" She trailed off and stared at him in bewilderment. "What's wrong?"

Senior citizens. There it was again, the target group of her scams—and right here in this neighborhood. He shuddered to think that the "library fund" money might end up right in Mari Lamott's pocket. And that somebody might find out and then she'd be in big trouble and he had done nothing to stop it.

"Honey, do you mean to tell me that you just go around ringing doorbells and asking for money with no ID or anything?"

Mari nodded slowly. "Almost everybody knows me. I'm usually the one who goes around the neighborhood for the heart drive and the school band sales and the Scouts. I started the Neighborhood Watch program around here, so I've been in everyone's home."

Worse and worse! She had scoped out every house near her already. She was trouble waiting to happen. How could someone who looked and acted so sweet and innocent be so unscrupulous about money? It was almost as if she were two different people.

"Oh, my," Mari said with dismay. "I can see that you don't think it's a good idea at all. I'm sure that other women probably don't do stuff like this, but I *like* meeting people. Well, older people. I guess I'm not that comfortable with people my own age."

"No, other women do *not* do stuff like this," he

assured her, but he meant something entirely different from what she was thinking. "Look, give me a minute to eat the sandwich and wash my hands, and I'll come with you."

"You will?" She brightened perceptibly.

"Yes, God help me, I will," he said with slightly more enthusiasm than he felt. He could see that he was going to have to stick to her like a pair of polyester pants two sizes too small. He had promised his grandmother, after all, and though he hated to admit it, he sort of liked Mari himself. She was funny and surprising and cute. So, tired as he was, he was going to see her through this little neighborhood foray. After all, how many people could she really know?

She knew a lot of people, an *awful* lot of people, Patrick found out. At the end of three hours, his feet were hot, his throat was dry, and he had the beginnings of a really bad headache. Mari, on the other hand, was disgustingly cheerful, having collected one hundred, eighty-nine dollars and seventy-five cents, most of it in cash. It seemed as if everyone over the age of sixty within a three-mile radius of her shop knew her.

Patrick's arms were laden with the small gifts several people had pressed upon her—a tiny potted African violet, some homemade cookies, a lace-edged handkerchief. He had suggested that they drive his car, but Mari had wanted to walk. "They sit out on their porches," she'd said. "It's a treat for them to see someone walking in the neighborhood."

"Are we done?" he asked as they headed in the general direction of the shop. "Or are you planning on canvassing Canada while you're at it?"

Mari laughed. "I think we're done. Are you hungry?"

"Starved." He glanced at his watch. "Damn. I've got to be at the ball field in half an hour."

She looked disappointed, but she said, "You go on, then. I'll just run the money over to the night depository at my bank. I can write a check for the library on Monday. And thank you so much for your help."

But Patrick wasn't done yet. He wasn't about to leave Mari and the money alone together for too long. Temptation was the last thing she needed.

"Tell you what," he said. "What if you come to the game with me? We can get a hot dog there."

"Sounds nice." She was smiling again.

Now there was one more problem to solve. All of the kids on the team knew that he was a cop. And he could bet that they would be tripping over themselves to talk to Mari.

"There is one other thing," he said. "Sort of an image problem."

She looked at him quizzically.

"The kids think… That is, I told them that I'm a…cop."

Mari stopped walking and stared at him in disbelief. "You lied to them?"

He felt a moment of irritation, thinking that she was a fine one to talk about lying. But then, maybe she was one of those people who were pathological liars, who didn't really know the difference between a lie and the truth.

"I stretched the truth a bit," he said. "I used to be a security guard."

"But if you don't tell children the truth—" she began, and then she stopped and frowned. "Oh, it's that masseur thing again, isn't it?"

"Massage therapist," he corrected automatically.

"Maybe you do have a point. Kids might not understand about something like that. I mean, it's kind of an...erotic profession." She glanced at him for confirmation.

"Oh, it is that," he agreed.

"Well, I guess it's for the best. But why didn't you make up something else? I mean, couldn't you have told them that you're a bus driver?"

"A cop's more of an authority figure," he said. "The kids tend to be a little more respectful toward me."

"I see your point. But you are going to tell them the truth sometime, aren't you?"

"Oh, I definitely believe the truth is a good idea."

Patrick could hardly concentrate on the game. Mari was perched on the bleachers in her little white shorts and pink top right next to some older woman. And they were talking. Actually they'd been talking for the last hour of the game. Patrick could see that the woman was laughing, and he wondered what Mari had told her.

"Coach?" a kid beside him on the bench asked hesitantly, clearing his throat. The boy had to repeat the word before Patrick quit staring at Mari to glance down at Davy. It took him another moment to realize that he was in the middle of a ball game. His nine-year-old boys had been remarkably quiet during the game, a rarity that he knew was because of his own preoccupation.

"Coach, Andrew wants to know if you're gonna let him bat. He thinks he should get a chance like everybody else."

Patrick sighed. Andrew never spoke for himself unless it was to swear, which was why he was out of the lineup tonight. In the middle of the last game, he had let the umpire know in no uncertain terms what he thought of being struck out.

"Davy, are you Andrew's designated talker?"

Davy didn't understand at first, then he sighed. "No," he said. "He was—I mean, I was just wondering."

Patrick had given up trying to be overt about his worry. Now he shaded his eyes as he studied the stands. Beside him, Davy assumed the same pose.

"Coach?" Davy asked. "You got a girlfriend up there?"

"What?" Patrick was so startled that he stepped sideways, almost into the water bucket.

"Well, I just wanted you to know that I know what it's like," Davy advised. "I had a girlfriend last year, but she kept doing stupid things like trying to kiss me, so I had to let her go. I know how it is."

Davy went back to the bench to sit down, and Patrick turned back to the game. But he couldn't keep his mind on it. Going through his head were all of the possible things Mari and the older woman could be discussing. Social security checks and insurance money were high on his list.

He had another problem on his hands. Just what was he supposed to tell people that Mari was? His girlfriend, as Davy had surmised? His grandmother's friend? He guessed that for now he'd better just stick to introducing her as his friend. And she was that, albeit a friend in dire need of guidance.

But he had other friends who had been in the same boat. There were any number of small-time would-be crooks he had more or less rehabilitated in some small way. There were shoplifters and drunks and forgers who had enough decency in their souls that they wanted to live a moral life. And he had helped them out, gotten them into treatment programs, lent them money or gotten them small, respectable jobs.

That whole line of thought gave him an idea. He could introduce Mari to some of these people and maybe she would see that it was possible to live a full life without scamming some poor senior citizen. He knew one person he could call right off the bat. Once he explained things to him, he knew he would be more than willing to help him work with Mari.

He was so cheered by that thought that he clapped his hands when the next out was made, which, unfortunately, was an out for his team. Davy looked up at him from the bench and shook his head mournfully. "He's got a girlfriend," he whispered to Andrew.

By the time the game ended, Patrick's headache had taken on a life of its own. He'd been too busy keeping an eye on Mari to eat anything. Now his stomach churned and his head throbbed. There was a dull red haze emanating from somewhere behind his eyes, so that Mari looked as if she were climbing down from the bleachers in a fog at sunset. He rubbed his temples, murmuring what he hoped were congratulatory words to the boys and their parents as they left.

"What have you gotten into now?" he asked without prelude when Mari stood in front of him, and everyone else had gone.

Mari frowned. "What's wrong? You've got a headache, don't you? Those hot dogs are stuffed with nitrates, you know." She fished in her purse. "Here, I always carry some raisins in case I need something to eat."

He made a growling sound of exasperation deep in his throat, leaving Mari to conclude that carrying around raisins was another of those things that most women didn't do. She closed her purse and waited for him to explain.

"Whose grandmother was that?" he asked, bracing himself for the worst.

"She said her grandson's name is Davy. He's the shortstop."

Patrick groaned. "And when are you going to see her again?"

"How did you know I was going to see her again?"

"Because the universe is playing a cosmic joke on me."

Mari wasn't sure what that meant, but given his mood, it didn't seem like something she should question. She took a deep breath. "She wants me to come over tomorrow for lunch. She's having friends in and she thinks they'd get a kick out of me doing a..." She cleared her throat, knowing how he would react to this next piece of news. "Doing a reading for them."

He didn't disappoint her, uttering an expletive she didn't remember ever hearing in public before.

"How much is she going to pay you?" he demanded from between clenched teeth.

"Patrick, you know I don't do this for money," she

protested, but it was useless. He fixed her with a hard stare and she sighed. "She's going to make a donation to the library fund. I told her she didn't have to do that, but she insisted."

"I bet she did," he said darkly. He didn't know whether to hunt down Davy's grandmother and throttle her for having such little sense or to throttle Mari instead on general principles. At the moment his headache didn't make either option really viable.

He couldn't remember having such an aggravating day, not even when he'd had to chase a car thief through a car wash and then across a field of Canada thistles. Even wet and stuck with thorns, he hadn't felt like this, as if every second today had been a personal test of his sanity.

"Come on," Mari said soothingly. "Let me take you home and fix you some dinner. I owe you at least that for the muffler."

How could a diabolical little she-devil sound so sweet? he wondered through his throbbing headache. But he allowed her to lead him off the field and to his car.

Her apartment was cool, and his headache eased somewhat, especially after she insisted on making him a cold compress with a cloth and some ice. He dropped his car keys onto the counter, then sat at her kitchen table and wondered how he was going to stick with her the rest of the weekend until he made sure she gave the money to the library on Monday. It had become a point of honor with him. Once Patrick Keegan had set his sights on a would-be criminal, he didn't let up for a minute. And this little lady was the grand master of all potential criminals, as far as he was concerned.

Mari fried hamburgers and set them in front of Patrick along with potato chips. "What do you want to drink?" she asked.

"How about some cold milk?"

She fidgeted. "Sorry, no milk. I'm lactose intolerant. But there's Kool-Aid and beer in the refrigerator and lots of other alcohol in the cabinet."

He couldn't face hard alcohol right now any more than he could face Kool-Aid. And she looked so hopeful that he couldn't bring himself to ask for plain water.

"Beer sounds good."

"Want some ice with it?" she asked.

He would have smiled if his head didn't still hurt. "No, honey, just the can's fine."

The beer was light, but he gamely drank it anyway. Mari got him a couple of aspirin, and fifteen minutes later his head felt much better. But he was still so tired that he was ready to fall face-first into the potato chips.

Mari had turned on the news, and Patrick stumbled to his feet, thinking of nothing more than getting home to his bed. He would worry about Mari and the grandmothers and Mari and the library money tomorrow.

His car keys weren't on the counter where he could have sworn he left them, and he looked around for a minute before he noticed that Mari was studiously staring at the TV, though the screen was showing an ad for patio furniture.

"Have you seen my car keys?"

"No."

Her answer was a little too quick. And she wouldn't look at him. "All right," he said. "What's going on?"

Mari was chewing on her lip now. "I'm afraid I can't let you drive," she said quietly.

"What are you talking about?"

"I hid your car keys. You're impaired."

"I'm *what?*" He stalked toward her, but she stood and went behind the couch, putting it between them.

"I'm sorry," she said. "But I'm going to have to put my foot down about this."

"I had one light beer," he said, appealing to her reason—if she had any. "That's hardly enough to impair a driver."

"Maybe not. But you're dead tired, you have a headache, and I don't want to have to come bail you out of jail if some officer stops you, smells beer on your breath and decides to haul you off." She had had enough experience bailing out her sister to consider being hauled off a real possibility.

"Nobody's going to haul me off to jail," he said, edging closer to her.

She scurried to the end of the couch. "That's another thing. I don't like to be critical, but sometimes you're a little overconfident."

"Am I?" He was beginning to smile.

"Yes." He had her worried now. He kept slowly walking around the couch until he was behind it, and she had edged to the front.

"You know, I am pretty confident about one thing," he told her. "I'm going to get those car keys from you."

Mari swallowed hard. "This is really for your own

good. I'm not in the habit of having men spend the
night in—''

She broke off with a squeak of alarm as he vaulted
the couch in one smooth move and caught her around
the waist. The next instant she was lying on her back
on the couch, and Patrick stood next to her, one knee
braced beside her waist, her wrists clasped in one of
his large hands.

"Now," he said, grinning, "what were you saying
about my overconfidence?''

"Patrick, let's negotiate," she said, her eyes wide.

"Oh, I don't think so, honey," he said with rich
amusement. "You see, it's a little late for that. I'm
afraid I'm going to have to search you."

She was chewing on her lip, but he could tell that
she wasn't really afraid of him. In fact, he could see
that despite her anxiety over his potentially impaired
driving, her eyes were soft with some other emotion.

"Now where would you hide my keys?" he wondered, eyeing her chest with growing interest.

"Patrick, really, I...I don't have them on me."

Patrick clucked his tongue. "Oh, don't think you
can weasel out of this now." With one hand, he began
to slowly lift her pink top, enjoying the way her
breathing changed. His hand explored her breasts
through her bra until Mari made a soft moaning sound.
Then he deftly unsnapped the bra with one hand and
pushed it up. Her nipples were already hard and he
savored them a moment before lowering his head to
tease them with his mouth. She arched beneath him
and her breath caught. He released her hands, and she
clutched his back.

Now he undid her jeans and lowered one hand to

explore there. He stroked her flat stomach, then inched lower until he was gently probing between her soft thighs.

Mari pressed herself against him, totally lost.

Patrick's own breathing was becoming more labored as he kissed and sucked her breasts. She had a beautiful body, soft and just curved enough to be exquisitely female. The valley between her breasts tasted sweet, and he spent considerable time kissing and nuzzling her there until she whimpered his name.

She was squirming against his hand that continued to stroke her between her legs, and Patrick's own jeans were now so uncomfortable that he nearly stripped them off right then and there.

He stopped himself abruptly when she whispered, "Please."

Mari's eyes were fever-bright and moist. Her mouth was parted, and her body trembled. Patrick had never seen a woman so willing and so responsive in such a short time. And never had one so sweetly and softly said "please" to him before. It was his undoing.

If she hadn't said that, he could have so easily lost himself in her body. He had forgotten who he was and what he was doing. He had forgotten that this was just a game to get his keys back. He had never lost his own control so quickly before, and it shook him.

His hands trembled slightly as he closed her jeans, then carefully pulled down her bra and top.

"Patrick, I'm...sorry," she whispered, her voice shaky.

"It's all right," he said more gruffly than he'd intended.

"I didn't mean to..." Her voice trailed off.

"You didn't do anything wrong, Mari," he told her, though he couldn't bring himself to meet her eyes. He blamed himself for what had happened. He had been so tired and aggravated that he had lost his control over the situation, but he wasn't going to tell her that. He didn't want her getting any ideas about the effect she had on him.

"I guess you want your car keys now," she said quietly, standing and looking so miserable that he wanted to put his arms around her.

Patrick shook his head. "You were right. I'm almost asleep on my feet. I think I'll spend the night on your couch, if it's okay with you."

He could see that that surprised her, but he had his reasons for staying. For one thing, he would be around to monitor her visit tomorrow to Davy's grandmother. And he would ensure that she didn't dip into the library money in the meantime.

"I'll get you a pillow and some covers."

She escaped the room in such a hurry that he knew she was embarrassed. He had to say something to her, but he didn't know what.

"Mari," he said gently when she dropped the pillow and blanket on the couch and started to retreat to the bedroom. She halted, and he turned her around to face him. "Mari, there's nothing to be embarrassed about. You didn't do anything wrong."

She sighed heavily. When her eyes met his, they were twin pools of worry. "That's just it," she said miserably. "I don't know what to do."

"You really haven't had any sexual experience?"

"Only Warren G. Harding. And he was more interested in my knees than anything else."

Patrick tried hard not to smile. "Warren G. Harding, the president?" he asked gently. "Surely you're not that old, honey."

She gave him a tiny smile and shook her head. "The band teacher. He was my only...lover. But I didn't like what he did. It never felt like it did when you touched me." She blushed furiously at this, and Patrick gently stroked her hair back.

"You see? It isn't you. It was old Warren G. *He* was the one who didn't know what he was doing. You, on the other hand, are in a different class altogether. It's obvious that you're a natural at sex."

"Me?" She looked so surprised that again he had to work at not smiling.

"Yes, you."

"You mean, I'm not a failure compared to the other women you know?"

"Not by any means. You may not know much about it, but that's all the better. You let yourself feel. And, believe it or not, a lot of women can't do that."

"Really?"

"Yes, really. Now I'm going to try to get some sleep here, and I think you ought to do the same."

Mari nodded. She started toward the bedroom, then stopped and turned back to him hesitantly.

"Patrick, do you think that maybe sometime we could...do more than we did tonight?"

"You mean, go all the way?"

She nodded.

No other woman had ever posed the question quite that way, and he found that her insecurity and honesty warmed him. "Normally, I'd take you up on that in-

vitation right away, but I'm a little tuckered out tonight. Get some sleep, honey.''

He hadn't really answered her question, Mari realized as she closed the door to her bedroom. But the
prospect of going all the way with Patrick Keegan was
certainly the most exciting thing that had ever happened to her.

6

Mari was jolted out of a fitful sleep four hours later when the phone jangled. She caught it on the first ring, knowing even before she answered who would be calling her at two in the morning.

It was Mariette, in trouble again, fifty miles away in Masonfield.

"I don't know how this happened," she complained. "This cop pulled me over, and the next thing I knew he was taking me to the station about some traffic tickets. You've got to get me out of here, Mari."

"What about Harmon?" Mari asked, thinking that Mariette's boyfriend should certainly be the one to bail her out of her latest disaster.

Mariette sighed heavily. "He doesn't have any money, Mari. We're sort of between jobs."

Mari rubbed the skin between her eyebrows where a headache was beginning to form.

"How much money do you need, for bail and whatever else?" she asked in resignation.

Mariette told her, and Mari groaned. That would take every cent she had saved for her upcoming vacation. Of course she never planned anything too big for her vacation, maybe a short trip to Indianapolis and some museums. But now that she was the new, exciting Mari, she had dared to hope that she might do something more interesting this vacation, like stay at a lodge in Wisconsin. But the Wisconsin lodge dream was going up in smoke in the face of Mariette's latest crisis.

"I'll be there as soon as I can," Mari said, suppressing another sigh.

She slipped on her clothes as quietly as she could in the dark, then tiptoed into the living room. Patrick was still sound asleep on the couch, lying on his side with his arm trailing down to the floor. Just her luck, Mari thought. The one time in her life that she had a good-looking man spending the night in her apartment, and she had to go rescue her sister.

Mari crept into the kitchen and carefully pulled out the bottom drawer beside the stove. She fished around under the pile of napkins until she found the emergency money she kept for Mariette's late-night rescues and Mari's vacations—if she ever got one. She stuffed the money into her purse, then stole one last, longing look at Patrick before she slipped down the stairs and out the door.

Patrick's car was behind hers, but she was able to pull on down the alley and get out that way. It was an hour's drive to the jail where Mariette was, and Mari rehearsed her speech the entire way. *I can't come bail you out of every scrape. From now on you're responsible for your own mistakes.*

Harmon was waiting at the police station entrance. He was bare-chested with a ring through one pierced nipple. Mari tried not to stare as she gave him the money. She sat down on the bench just inside the front door and leaned back against the cool wall, closing her eyes. She had lived this scene over and over from the time she was a teenager. She had waited for Mariette outside the principal's office and the school detention room in high school and then in the receiving area of the local jail in almost every town within driving distance of Mari's home.

Mariette never got into serious trouble; it was always something petty. And it seemed that all she had to do was bat her big brown eyes at the judge and she got off with a warning. While Mari knew that if she so much as dropped a candy wrapper on the ground she'd have security swarming all over her. She had the same brown eyes, but she just didn't have the knack of using them.

She sat up straight and opened her eyes as a heavy door closed. Mari's jaw dropped when she saw Mariette walking toward her. She was dressed in high heels and a man's T-shirt that clearly showed that she wore no bra. The shirt just touched the tops of her thighs, making Mari wonder if she was wearing any underpants, either. And wrapped around her neck was the most ridiculous, cheap-looking boa that shed pink feathers with every step she took.

"You saved my life!" Mariette cried in typical dramatic fashion, rushing to her sister and hugging her tightly. "Oh, God! There was a hooker in my cell."

"Speaking of hookers," Mari said dryly, disentangling herself and plucking a feather from her mouth. "What are you doing dressed like that?"

Mariette grinned sheepishly. "Harmon and I were

a little short on cash this week, so I took a temporary job dancing at this club.''

Mari's eyebrows went up. "What club?"

"Calm down. It's perfectly legal. Well, at least that's what the owner told me. Technically, I'm not nude. I wear pasties and a G-string—and this boa.''

"Well, that's certainly a far cry from nude," Mari said sarcastically.

"Oh, lighten up. I was making great tips. And then tonight some customer said there was going to be a raid because there was some illegal crap game going on in back. So I lit out of there with Harmon on his motorcycle.''

"Which would explain why you're wearing his shirt," Mari guessed.

"Exactly. Only we got pulled over, and the cop was going to cite me for indecent exposure or something, and then he found out about the traffic tickets. And now the motorcycle's in the impound garage.''

"Well, I hope you and Harmon have a happy life together," Mari said, turning for the door.

"Mari! Wait! Where are you going?"

"Home. I might even have a drink when I get there. Don't look so surprised. I'm not the same Mari Lamott you remember.''

"Hey, it's only been a couple of weeks since I left," Mariette said.

"A lot can happen in a couple of weeks," Mari told her. "I assure you that I'm a whole new woman." She started for the door again, then stopped and sighed. "All right. I'll drop you and Harmon wherever you're staying. And then I'm going home. And you aren't going to call me the next time you get in trouble. Understand?''

"Sure, Mari," Mariette assured her, patting her arm and dislodging more pink feathers in the process. "No problem."

It was almost 6:00 a.m. when Mari arrived back home. She maneuvered her car until she got it as close as she could to where it was parked the night before. Brushing off the last of the pink feathers clinging to her clothes, she got out and shut the door as quietly as possible. The Sunday newspaper was sitting on the step, and she took it inside with her.

She was especially proud of herself when she made it almost to the top of the stairs in her apartment without making a sound. There was faint light from the morning sun, and Mari could make out Patrick's shadowy form on the couch. She stepped into the living room and immediately something grabbed her around the ankle. Mari gave a loud squeak of surprise before she realized that it was Rex playing his favorite game. Patrick made a low sound and rolled onto his back just as Rex made his escape, bounding onto the arm of the couch and from there to Patrick's stomach.

Mari watched in horror as Patrick sat bolt upright, muttering something that, had she been able to understand it, probably would have been obscene. Rex stared back at Patrick, wide-eyed, and uttered an innocent meow. Patrick swore again, and this time Mari had no trouble understanding it. She winced and rushed to get Rex.

But the cat wasn't tired of the game yet, and he

jumped to the floor and made a beeline for the bathroom. Mari watched helplessly, then turned to Patrick.

"I'm sorry," she said. "He gets wound up in the morning."

"Morning?" he asked groggily. "I thought it was the middle of the night." He blinked hard, then frowned at Mari. "What are you doing up already?"

"I...went to get the newspaper. I always look forward to the Sunday comics," she added lamely.

"You must be a hell of a 'Blondie' fan," he said dryly.

"Actually, it's 'Cathy.'" She shifted her weight. "I guess I ought to let you get back to sleep. I apologize for Rex."

"I'm awake now," he said around a yawn. "You wouldn't have any coffee, would you?"

"I was just about to make some." Actually she had been just about to go to bed. After less than four hours sleep, a middle-of-the-night rescue mission, and a close encounter with Rex, she was feeling less than peppy. But maybe coffee would help.

Half an hour later she had fallen asleep beside Patrick, her head on the couch arm and her feet curled under her bottom. Patrick took the pillow she'd given him the night before and tucked it gently under her head, then stretched out her feet until she looked more comfortable. He got up and poured himself more coffee. He was starting to feel hungry, and he remembered a little doughnut shop down the street.

Patrick was in the alley and about to head for the street on foot when it struck him that Mari's car wasn't exactly where she'd left it the night before. He frowned and went back to check it. The doors were locked, and he'd never known a car thief to return a car and lock it up. But something wasn't right here. He slowly circled the car, looking through the windows.

The only thing out of the ordinary he could see were three pink feathers lying on the seat.

Patrick shook his head and walked away.

Mari slowly opened her eyes and blinked. For a moment she didn't know why she was lying on the couch. Then she realized that she must have fallen asleep and nearly leaped to her feet in one movement. Rex, who had been curled at her back, sat up in alarm.

She blinked again and saw Patrick sitting in the chair leaning forward and peering intently at the TV. The sound was off, and he was apparently trying to follow a golf tournament.

"He's putting for an eagle," he said without looking over at her.

"How long have I been asleep?" she asked, trying to straighten her hair and read the clock at the same time.

"About five hours," he said conversationally. "You must not have slept well last night."

"I…I tossed and turned a lot. Too much Kool-Aid, I guess." She stood, twisting her hands together. "You can turn up the sound now, if you want."

He shook his head. "No thanks. I can't stand sports commentators. I end up getting into arguments with them."

"You're saying you argue with the TV?"

"Yeah, that's pretty much what I'm saying. There

are some doughnuts on the table. Hope you like bear claws.''

Mari edited her comment about the fat in doughnuts and went to the table to poke into the bag. She had a feeling that Patrick had more on his mind than the silent golf tournament, and it probably had something to do with the fact that she had just conked out for five hours after supposedly spending eight hours in bed.

''I guess I was pretty tired,'' she said hesitantly.

''Hiking the neighborhood getting library donations can do that to a person.''

He didn't sound convinced, and Mari felt compelled to add, ''I forgot to take my vitamins yesterday. I bet that's it.''

''Probably,'' Patrick agreed as Mari watched him from the corner of her eye. She still didn't think he believed her, but she didn't know what else to say.

For his part, Patrick was sure she was hiding something, but for now he had no idea what it was. All he had to go on were the facts that the car had been moved and there were pink feathers on the seat. He couldn't draw any obvious conclusions from that. And the library money was still intact. He had checked on it while Mari was sleeping. Once he made sure that Mari delivered it to the library on Monday, he could concentrate on rehabilitating Mari into an upstanding citizen.

''Davy's grandmother is expecting me for lunch,'' Mari said hesitantly. ''I guess I'd better go to the bedroom and change.''

''I'm going with you,'' Patrick announced.

''I really...I mean...'' Suddenly it dawned on her

that he meant to Davy's grandmother's house and not to the bedroom. "Oh! Well, you really don't have to go."

"I know that. But I need to talk to Davy's grandmother about…his hitting."

Mari's brows went up. It was such an obvious ploy that she was surprised he had tried it. "His hitting," she repeated.

Patrick cleared his throat. "I like to bring the family in on the team's progress."

"Oh, you are such a liar," she said, shaking her head. "Honestly, do you expect me to believe that?"

"And why not?" he asked a little indignantly, thinking that if anyone deserved to be called a liar here, she was the prime candidate.

"Because I know what you're up to."

"You do?" For a moment he thought that she had somehow found out that he was a cop.

"Of course I do. You're still worried that I'll say something inappropriate about your being a masseur when everyone from the team thinks you're a cop."

"Massage therapist."

"Right." She shook her head slowly. "See? You're even defensive about your job title. It's obvious that you have a problem with your self-image. You have an identity crisis."

"Obvious, is it?" he asked, trying not to show his amusement.

Mari nodded emphatically. "I'll admit that a massage therapist has a bit of a New Age feel about it. It's even—what do the kids say?—out there. But there's no need for you to feel embarrassed about what you do. We need to work on that."

Patrick couldn't help himself. He began to laugh while Mari regarded him with patient tolerance, obviously convinced that he was still suffering from his identity crisis.

"I'm sorry," he said at last. "But I don't think anyone's ever offered to boost my self-image for me before."

"No doubt," Mari said. "You act like you have an overabundance of self-confidence. A big ego. But that's really a cover-up. People sometimes act the opposite of what they're really like inside. Any psychologist will tell you that."

"Really?" he said. He was enjoying listening to her expound on his psychological profile. One thing he could say for Mari—he'd never been at a loss for amusement in the short time he'd known her. "Does this extend to sexual behavior, as well?"

"What?" That stopped her in her tracks. She chewed her lower lip as she watched him.

"What about the kind of man who sets out to seduce a woman? What does that say about him?" He didn't know why he felt compelled to tease her like this, but he was having a hell of a good time doing it. And he really enjoyed watching her chew that soft little lip.

"Well," she said carefully, "it might say that he's insecure about himself as a man."

Patrick clicked his tongue as if that were a sad state of affairs for a man.

"Or," she went on hesitantly, "it could mean that he finds the woman very attractive."

Patrick nodded solemnly. "You don't say."

Mari frowned. "Are you saying that you're thinking about seducing me?" she demanded.

"Sweetheart, I thought this was a hypothetical discussion about my self-image."

"Oh, no, you don't. Don't pull that innocent stuff on me. It hasn't worked since I was twelve. Now, were you talking about seducing me or not?"

He could see that he had her total attention now. She was watching him with wide eyes, and the lip chewing had slowed.

"Well, now, I'm not sure," he said, pretending to consider. "Maybe it was just one of those subconscious things that slipped out. I've been giving a lot of massages to women lately."

Mari frowned again. "Then you were thinking about seducing someone, but you're not sure who?"

"Maybe that's it," he said, nodding slowly.

"Oh. It's probably your poor self-image. You can't commit to seducing a particular woman because of fear of failure."

"Is that a fact?" he asked, working to look serious. "I guess I should forget the whole idea."

She looked so disappointed that he had a hard time not smiling. "But then again," he said, rubbing his chin, "maybe I should work through this self-image thing. Maybe I should think a little more about this seducing business. Just in theory, of course."

"Of course," she said, looking even more crestfallen.

He waited another few seconds, then said, "If it's in my subconscious, maybe the best thing to do would be to act on it. You know, get it out in the open. Explore the possibilities. Get some practice."

"That sounds like a good plan," she said warily.

"Of course I'd need someone to practice on. A woman."

Mari nodded. She looked hopeful now. "Maybe someone not too experienced," she suggested. "Just to make sure your ego doesn't get trampled."

Patrick couldn't hold back his smile any longer. "Maybe somebody who hasn't been with a man since Warren G. Harding."

Mari blushed. "Really? You're going to seduce me? Now?"

Patrick laughed. "A good seduction can't be rushed. And we have to get to Davy's grandmother's house."

Mari looked disappointed, but she nodded. She started for the bedroom, then stopped. "This seduction," she said slowly. "Do you have any idea when…"

Patrick's eyes glittered with devilment. "You can't make an appointment for a seduction," he said. "That would spoil all the fun. You'll just have to wait and see."

Patrick chuckled softly to himself as she disappeared into the bedroom. He had started the whole conversation about seduction as a game. After all, he wasn't in the habit of seducing women he'd known for such a short time, especially women on the wrong side of the law.

But he was definitely looking forward to seducing little Mari Lamott. She was sweet and soft and sexy, and she stirred emotions he didn't even know he had.

Patrick was used to a fairly active sex life, but he had his standards, and lately the women he normally preferred had lost some of their appeal. He liked curvy party girls who'd been around the world and who didn't want commitment any more than he did. He had a feeling that Mari hadn't even been around the block—at least sexually. And, as for partying, any woman who found her excitement in Kool-Aid didn't get to many parties.

Still, every time she looked at him with those soulful brown eyes, he felt an ache in his groin.

Davy's grandmother's name was Thelma, and she lived in a downtown apartment complex. She had invited two of her neighbors for lunch, Lucille and Opal. They all thanked Mari effusively for the plate of brownies she had brought, made a five-dollar donation to the library fund, then invited Patrick and Mari to sit at the small kitchen table. It was a tight squeeze, but Patrick sat next to Mari on one side, leg to leg and shoulder to shoulder.

Mari had dressed for the occasion since she knew she was supposed to give a reading. She had raided Mariette's closet again, taking a pair of lightweight blue leggings and pairing them with an oversize, blue cotton tunic top. She wore silver hoops at her ears and had dared to brush on some blue eye shadow and mascara. One of Mariette's hot-pink lipsticks completed the makeup, and Mari had found herself staring into the mirror at the exciting, provocative Mari Lamott she had come to enjoy impersonating.

Mari complimented Thelma on the pork roast, dressing, mashed potatoes and homemade rolls, then asked her a few questions about Davy until Thelma was telling them one story after another, pride in her voice.

Patrick had been to enough of his own grandmother's planned luncheons to know that this was *special occasion* food, even if Mari didn't. This was the kind of meal that grandmothers fixed when they wanted their grandchild to do something that they suspected the grandchild would not want to do. It was the kind of lunch his grandmother had fixed him before she announced that if he was set on becoming a cop, then he should get a college education so he would be a smart cop. And she had talked him into it over roast beef and her famous sweet-potato casserole.

"I'm so excited about getting you to do a reading," Thelma said, spooning more mashed potatoes onto Mari's plate. "Lucille and Opal and I pool some money every week to play that multistate lottery. So maybe if you could get some idea what numbers we should pick, it would really help."

Mari smiled weakly. "The lottery isn't my strong suit when it comes to doing readings," she said hesitantly. "I'd hate to think you were betting your money on numbers I recommended."

"Oh, don't worry, dear," Thelma said, winking at her. "We don't spend much on the lottery. We save our gambling for pinochle."

If Thelma thought that that would reassure Mari, she was wrong. "Surely you don't want me to predict your pinochle games," Mari protested.

"Not at all," Thelma assured her. Lucille and Opal were nodding at each word Thelma said, giving Mari the impression that Thelma was the official spokeswoman for the trio. "Although maybe I shouldn't tell you where we play, just so the detective here doesn't raid us." She winked again, and Mari shot Patrick an

I-told-you-so look. He smiled back as if he were totally unconcerned about their misconception as to his vocation.

"Would you like some more tea, dear, before we get started?" Thelma asked solicitously.

But Mari just wanted to get the so-called reading over with. It was difficult enough to do this with Patrick along for the ride, not to mention having to worry at the same time about Patrick's low self-esteem where his job was concerned.

"I think I'd like to get to the reading," Mari said, repressing a sigh.

"Oh, goody," Thelma cried. "Where do you want to go?"

Back home, Mari thought, barely restraining herself from saying it out loud.

"This table will be fine if we clear it off."

Patrick and Mari helped the women clear the dishes, and then Mari sat with the tarot cards she had found in Mariette's drawer while she was looking for the tunic top.

With a significant glance at Patrick, who stood leaning against the sink, Mari handed the cards to Thelma to shuffle. When she got them back she began to deal them out to the women as if they were about to play poker. Patrick, ducked his head to hide a grin. She was so obviously incompetent at this that he had grown fond of watching her inept performances.

"We're planning on going to Las Vegas next month," Thelma said. "Tell us how we should bet our money."

The first card that Mari turned over in front of

Thelma read Temperance and Mari was encouraged by that.

"You should tread lightly in all matters financial," she said with a shake of her head. "Don't wager more than you can afford to lose."

Thelma's mouth dropped in disappointment. "Does that temperance pertain to everything?" she wondered.

Mari nodded. "Especially to alcoholic drinks and the buffets."

Behind her, Patrick sounded as if he was choking, but when she looked, he was running water into a glass.

The first card Mari turned over in front of Lucille showed a traveler walking past a long row of golden cups.

"Well, it looks like Lucille can drink on the trip," Thelma announced.

"I don't think so," Mari told her. "Those cups all look empty."

"Maybe it means she drank them all," Thelma offered.

Patrick seemed to be choking again, and Mari turned just in time to see him run more water.

Mari shook her head. "If I were you, I'd be very wary of alcohol in Las Vegas. Maybe you should stick to the dinner shows. Or even go someplace else altogether."

But Thelma was having none of that. "Let's see what the rest of the cards say," she suggested.

Opal's card said Wheel of Fortune and Thelma pounced on that. "Well, I guess maybe here's a sign we should play roulette."

"My intuition tells me it means you should stay in

your room watching that TV show," Mari said, causing all three women to sigh unhappily.

Mari did the same with each succeeding card. She managed to interpret every one of them as a warning to avoid gambling or alcohol or large crowds or—and this one really had Patrick choking—topless floor shows. By the time she had turned over the last card, Thelma was eyeing her suspiciously.

"You know, Mari," she said, "I almost think you're against anyone having a good time."

"Oh, no, nothing like that," Mari protested. "I just think a person should be careful. Especially with money."

"Tell you what," Thelma said. "We'll go to Las Vegas, and we'll watch the calories and stay away from nudie shows, but—" She stopped to point her finger at Mari. "There's no way I'm not putting five bucks on red at the roulette table."

"And I'm having a whiskey sour," Opal told Mari, startling everyone with her sudden burst of speech. "I really enjoyed that on the cruise we took."

"Just have a good time," Mari told them, packing up the cards and feeling great relief at having survived the reading. She noticed that the three women were exchanging glances. A second later Opal elbowed Lucille, who then cleared her throat and looked pointedly at Thelma.

Thelma took a deep breath and asked, "Wasn't that the kittens I just heard?"

Opal and Lucille immediately confirmed that yes, they thought that was the kittens. Mari hadn't heard anything.

Thelma left the room and returned with a box containing three kittens, two white and one gray, peering over the side. Opal and Lucille crooned to them as Thelma set the box on the table.

"Such a shame to have to let the janitor dispose of them," she said.

"Dispose of them?" Mari asked, alarm in her voice.

"Oh, we can't have pets in the building, dear," Thelma said. "Somebody must have dumped these off here. Opal found them crying so pitifully out by the Dumpster. They're so sweet, aren't they? But rules are rules."

"But he can't just…get rid of them," Mari said.

"I'm afraid the management is very insistent," Thelma said. "We hate to think of them being…eliminated, but what can we do? We can't keep them here."

There was a long moment of silence, broken finally by Mari's heavy sigh. "I suppose I could take them and try to find them homes," she said in resignation.

Thelma beamed. "Oh, that would be wonderful! Now why don't we all have some cake?"

Mari glanced at Patrick, and he rolled his eyes.

As he drove her back home later, the box of kittens on the back seat, Mari finally broke the silence between them.

"I know you think I'm crazy," she said, "but I couldn't let the janitor get rid of those poor little kittens."

Patrick just shook his head in disbelief. Mari was the most pitiful con artist he had ever seen. Here she had just been scammed by three grandmothers into taking home unwanted kittens. And that so-called reading… She could have given those three little old ladies her driver's license numbers to play in Las Vegas, and they would have been thrilled. But, no, she had to warn them against drinking and gambling and generally having a good time. She was mixing her bumbling psychic readings with her own personal temperance crusade.

She was the only con artist he knew who had a strict moral code.

"You're not saying anything," she ventured.

"I'm considering whether I should strangle you now or later."

"Does that mean you're not going to seduce me?"

"Not until you relocate those kittens. It's going to be damaging enough to my concentration to work on a seduction with one cat watching, much less another three."

Mari smiled then. "Maybe you could take them to the YMCA?"

Patrick just gave her a look.

7

Patrick spent that Sunday night parked outside Mari's shop, far enough down the street that she wouldn't see his car, but close enough that he would see if she left.

Her car stayed where she'd parked it all night, and in the morning he showed up at her doorstep to take her for coffee and then to the library to turn over the money.

It annoyed Patrick that the librarian behind the counter was male and that apparently he knew Mari well. It didn't escape Patrick's notice that the boy smiled at Mari an awful lot and thanked her profusely for the money and that Mari smiled back. Mari explained on the way out that she used to give him piano lessons. That annoyed Patrick, too, and he wasn't sure why.

It certainly wasn't because he was jealous. No, it wasn't that at all. Mari might be cute as all get-out, and her inept larceny amused him more than irritated him, but he had no emotional entanglements where she was concerned. He figured his irritation at her smiling at the boy librarian was because he had announced to her that he intended to seduce her, and here she was letting some boy make goo-goo eyes at her right under his nose.

He let her know about it over the coffee, and she stared at him in surprise.

"But all he did was smile at me," she protested. "That's hardly an invitation to go to bed with him."

"But that's exactly what he was thinking," he assured her, leaning back and crossing his arms over his chest.

"Really?"

He could see that she wasn't properly worried about the alleged goo-goo eyes, so he decided to try another approach.

"The fact of the matter is, if I'm going to seduce a woman, I want her to be focused on me and me alone."

Mari chewed on her lip. "Is this something peculiar to your low self-esteem or is it a male thing in general?"

Patrick was mildly annoyed by her failure to take him seriously on this matter. He frowned and narrowed his eyes. "I'm just trying to give you some guidelines on this," he told her.

"Is that what other women do?" she asked. "Confine their attention to only one man?"

"Generally, they confine it to one at a time anyway."

"Well, that sounds okay." Her mouth quirked up in a mischievous smile. "I'll try to remember to only smile invitingly at one man at a time."

Patrick couldn't believe that she was giving him a hard time over this. "I'd appreciate it," he said irritably.

He thought that she might have giggled then, but when he frowned at her sternly, she ducked her head and patted her mouth with her napkin. It probably hadn't been a giggle, he told himself. She was just nervous about this seduction thing.

Patrick dropped Mari at her shop, then went to work. He still felt dead tired after his weekend of sleeping inside and then outside of Mari's apartment. But all traces of tiredness vanished when he got his first phone call.

"Keegan?" the man asked. "This is Sergeant Del Stanley with the Masonfield police. We talked last week about some charges against a Mariette Lamott."

Patrick perked up immediately. "What have you got for me, Sergeant?"

"Just thought you might want to know that Miss Lamott was arrested Saturday night."

"What!"

"That's right. She was stopped for indecent exposure, but when the lieutenant found out about her outstanding traffic tickets he jailed her on that instead."

"Indecent exposure?" Patrick asked weakly.

"Seems she was pulled over as she left a club where she'd been waitressing tables and dancing in a...skimpy costume."

"What time was this?" Patrick ran an agitated hand through his hair. Surely Mari couldn't have driven over to Masonfield while he was sleeping and managed to get herself arrested. No way. It couldn't happen.

"The report says she was booked at 2:00 a.m."

Patrick groaned.

The sergeant laughed. "Let me tell you, that cell

was still a sight to see this morning, even after the janitor had gone. Pink feathers everywhere.''

"Pink feathers?" Patrick sounded as if he'd just been sucker punched.

"All over the place. I've been picking them off reports since I got here." He chuckled again.

"Tell me something," Patrick said. "Who bailed her out?"

"Harlon something-or-other," the sergeant said. "Don't have that in front of me. Probably someone from the club where she was. Hope I've been of help."

"Oh, you've been very helpful," Patrick assured him before he hung up. He sat there holding the coffee cup, staring into the inky brew that suddenly didn't seem strong enough. He had to face the fact that he was dealing with one very tricky little con artist here. She had snuck out in the middle of the night, right under his nose, and gotten herself into trouble fifty miles away. No wonder she'd been so tired in the morning.

He wondered if she moonlighted every weekend at the "club" in Masonfield. Well, that was going to stop right now. Patrick decided it was time to step up his rehabilitation program. He was going into high gear now, and Miss Mari Lamott was going to turn her life around or suffer the consequences.

He tried to summon a mental picture of how surprised she was going to look when she eventually found out just who he was, but the only image that came to mind was a seductive Mari covered in pink feathers. He slammed down his cup so hard that coffee sloshed onto the nearby papers.

* * *

Patrick camped outside Mari's apartment that night and the next, but her car stayed parked in the alley. He drank warm sodas and cold coffee as he stared up at her apartment windows, wondering what she was doing. He almost smiled as he pictured her pouring a glass of Kool-Aid. He caught sight of her once as she crossed in front of the window in shorts and a tank top. He bumped his head on the windshield straining for a better look.

He hit pay dirt on Wednesday evening when she came out the front door of the shop and got into her car. Patrick ducked down out of sight, then carefully pulled his car onto the street and kept a discreet distance behind her. She was headed in the direction of the highway, and he clutched the steering wheel tighter, wondering if she was on her way to Masonfield to dance on tables again in her pink feathers.

But she turned off at the Sunset Acres Rest Home, the same place he'd followed her to the previous Wednesday. Patrick watched her carry some papers inside, then gave her a ten-minute head start before he followed.

The receptionist looked up and smiled when she saw Patrick. "May I help you?"

"I'm looking for a little brunette who came in about ten minutes ago," he said.

"Oh, you must mean Mari. She's in the recreation room." The receptionist gave him directions, then watched with undisguised interest as he headed down the hall.

Patrick could hear a piano playing some ragtime tune, and he briefly wondered if someone had set up a stereo in the rec room. He came to a sudden stop in the doorway as he saw that it was a real piano and it was Mari doing the playing. Her eyes widened in surprise as she saw him, but she kept playing, although she began chewing her lip at the same time.

Patrick remembered that she had told him she played the piano and violin—along with the zither when it wasn't in the repair shop—but this wasn't what he had pictured. He had thought that she probably played classical pieces since she taught music. He just hoped that she didn't do any piano playing at the place where she danced half-naked on tables. Picturing her sitting at a piano in those pink feathers was nearly as unsettling as the mental image of her gyrating on a tabletop.

Patrick glanced around the room and saw about fifteen residents smiling and listening avidly, some of them clapping in time to the music. One older man was noticeably off the beat until the woman next to him elbowed him and loudly ordered him to adjust his hearing aid.

Mari ended the upbeat tune and turned nervously to Patrick. She was torn between happiness at seeing him and embarrassment at him finding her here in a nursing home. It wasn't exactly the prime setting for a fresh, exciting woman on the move.

"What are you doing here?" she demanded, and all of the eyes in the room turned to him.

"Has he got my pills?" someone demanded loudly.

Patrick realized that he had been so intent on catching Mari doing something illegal or at the least improper that he hadn't thought to invent an excuse for being here. It must be lack of sleep that was making him so addled. It certainly couldn't be Mari, even though she looked especially cute in short jean overalls. She had on a red T-shirt under it, and her hair was attractively disheveled.

It entered his mind that it definitely would be an enjoyable challenge to get her out of that outfit once they were alone, but he put that errant thought out of his mind before his libido got out of control.

"Do you give massages here?" Mari asked in a low voice.

Patrick shook his head. "No, I just came by to...check out the physical therapy facilities."

"Oh, but they're closed at night."

"Darn. Guess I'll just have to do it another time. But, since I'm here, maybe we could go somewhere when you're done."

"Sure." She smiled in pleasure.

"Play 'Strangers in the Night,'" a woman called.

Mari opened a music book and began to play, still darting glances toward Patrick. He finally took a seat near the back after a woman began tapping her cane and eyeing him suspiciously.

Mari played for a solid forty-five minutes, taking requests and getting the residents to sing along on several of the songs. When she quit, she mingled with them, touching a hand here and there and softly asking questions. Patrick noticed that most of the people in the room weren't very communicative, and he wondered why Mari did this. From the looks of things, there was no money to be had here. And precious little emotional reward.

Patrick had to face the fact that he could no longer believe that Mari was out to con senior citizens. From what he'd seen so far, just the opposite was true. But that didn't excuse her from her other law-breaking activities. He still had to get on with her rehabilitation— for her own good.

He started in on her as soon as they were in the parking lot, Mari with an armful of sheet music, which Patrick realized was what he had seen her carrying into the rest home the last time he'd followed her here.

"Why do you come here?" he asked bluntly.

"What?" She stared at him in surprise, obviously not expecting that particular question.

"Forgive me for saying so, but nobody in that room seemed particularly overjoyed at the visit. So why do it?"

Mari shook her head impatiently. "I'm not there for applause," she said, clearly indignant. "Those people all have memory problems, and most of them aren't socially responsive. Music is one thing that seems to awaken something in the brain. A couple of them never spoke a word since coming to the nursing home until they heard a song they'd listened to when they were young." The animation in Mari's face was so fetching that Patrick nearly forgot about her rehabilitation.

"The woman with the cane?" She put it in the tone of a question, and he nodded. "She didn't recognize her family when she first came to the home. Now she talks to everyone. And the man with the hearing aid has started eating well again. And taking walks." She had delivered all of this in a rush of words, and now she stopped suddenly, looking embarrassed.

"What's the matter?"

"You don't want to hear all of this," she said in a low voice.

To his own surprise, he did. But he wasn't going to press her on that issue when he had other things to cover with her. "I could listen to you talk about those people all night," he told her, "but you did say you'd go somewhere with me. So where are we going?"

Mari chewed her lip. She was supposed to go to church. She needed to pick up the new Sunshine Committee list, so she could get everybody organized before much longer. Choir practice was ending, so the church was open.

"You had other plans?" Patrick asked, wondering what her frown and all that lip chewing meant.

"Not exactly. But I need to stop somewhere first to pick up something."

But Patrick wasn't about to let her out of his sight after last Saturday night's episode in Masonfield. "I'll follow you to wherever you need to stop," he said firmly.

Mari hesitated, then decided she didn't have any choice. And she *had* to go to the church. "All right."

Patrick mentally went over the possibilities of where she might be headed as he followed her out of the lot. It was someplace she didn't especially want him to know about, so that narrowed the destinations. A bar? Did she work another shady avocation, as well? Or maybe the local tattoo parlor. He wouldn't put that past her, either. He just hoped she wasn't headed to some place where the people might know him and what he did for a living.

Well, that certainly didn't seem to be a possibility, Patrick admitted as Mari pulled into the parking lot of a church. He looked around to see if she actually might be going next door, but she parked close to the entrance. What was she up to now?

Mari ground her teeth as she got out of the car. She hadn't wanted Patrick to see her here, but there hadn't been a graceful way to get out of it. This was not where the cool, exciting women hung out.

"I'll just be a minute," Mari called to Patrick, but he was already shutting his car door and following her. She ground her teeth again and waited for him to catch up.

"So what are we doing here?" he asked.

"I have to pick up a list," she mumbled.

"What kind of list?"

"The Sunshine Committee," Mari said in a low voice, hoping he would think she was talking about a singles club. She pushed open the church door and hustled inside.

"Hi, Mari," the middle-aged female choir director said from the doorway to the sanctuary where she was turning out lights. "How were things at Sunset Acres?" The question trailed off as she spotted Patrick. "Well, I guess I'd better head on home. I'm all through here."

"This is Patrick Keegan, a friend," Mari said, not even sure that the director had heard as she disappeared through the outside door.

"Alone at last," Patrick said, raising his brows. "Do you always bring men here?"

"Hardly," Mari said, sighing. She hurried into the office on her left and picked up the committee list on the desk. She started for the door at a quick trot, but Patrick's hand on her arm stopped her.

"Honey, why are you trying to run out of here like your skirt's on fire?"

Mari couldn't quite meet his eyes. "I didn't think you'd be interested in hanging around here. It's not exactly...a swinging singles scene."

"Is that what you think I want?" he asked, frowning. "Come here and sit down a minute." He took her arm and guided her to one of the two chairs in front of the desk, then sat in the other one. "Now tell me what this list is you're getting. And don't leave out any details." He knew he sounded like a cop, but he was going to get a straight answer out of her one way or another.

Mari was staring at her shoes. "It's the list of who's on the Sunshine Committee," she said miserably.

"And what's so terrible about the Sunshine Committee?" he asked, just to set the record straight. "They aren't a terrorist group, are they?"

Mari glanced up at him and gave a small, worried smile. "No. Although I'm not sure about Mrs. Kurtz. She gets awfully upset if we miss somebody's birthday."

"So this committee is in charge of birthday greetings?" he guessed.

Mari nodded. "And get-well wishes. All of that kind of thing." She took a deep breath as if about to confess to a great crime. "I'm in charge of hospital admissions. I have to call the chaplain on duty there every day to see if any of our members have been admitted."

Patrick tried not to smile. She looked so contrite and anxious over this Sunshine Committee business that he was tempted to tease her about it. But he suspected that she would be crushed if he did. And she was chewing her lip again. It made him want to take her into his arms and kiss her until she smiled for him. It made him want to do all kinds of things to her that he shouldn't be thinking about at the moment.

"This doesn't sound too bad," he said gently. "Checking the hospital and sending cards and flowers. You know, honey, you had me worried that you were the leader of some senior citizens gang. You know, you spend an awful lot of time with people old enough to be your grandparents."

Mari did meet his eyes then, and he saw how truly miserable she was. He reached out immediately to take her hand and hold it in both of his.

"I guess I don't feel comfortable with people my own age," she said. "I grew up with mostly older people."

"Where did you grow up, honey? Florida?"

Mari shook her head. "Right here. But my mother was…an alcoholic. And my grandmother lived with us. I spent all of my time taking care of both of them." She carefully omitted mentioning her sister. She was sure that his opinion of her was low enough without the added burden of flighty, unreliable Mariette.

This explained a lot, Patrick thought. And maybe it was the reason she felt compelled to dance half-naked on tables and rack up traffic tickets. She had been forced into the role of an adult long before she was ready, and now she was sowing her wild oats. He just hoped she got the crop in before she got arrested.

"I guess you think I'm pretty boring," she said, lowering her eyes again.

"Actually, I think you're one of the most...interesting women I've ever met," he told her honestly.

"Really?" Her eyes brightened.

"Absolutely. I never knew anyone who drank Kool-Aid, and played piano for old people, and belonged to a Sunshine Committee. You're intriguing me all over again, honey."

Mari rolled her eyes at his blatant teasing, but she relaxed somewhat. She chewed her lip again and gave him a sly smile. "Does this mean you still want to seduce me?"

"Wild horses couldn't keep me from it now."

"Now? You mean right now?" She straightened in the chair and gave him a hopeful smile.

"Well, I..." Patrick began, completely undone by her candor. She certainly didn't take the coy route, and that was another thing he liked about her. "Actually, I think the surroundings would stifle my...creativity. Seducing a lady in church could probably get a man struck by lightning—or worse."

"Oh," she said with more than a trace of disappointment. "So you didn't come to Sunset Acres tonight to seduce me?"

That made Patrick smile. "Honey, I don't think I could carry off a seduction there any better than I could here. You hang around too many places that are off-limits to seduction, you know that?"

"Then why did you show up there?"

"Well, it turns out that I want to issue an invitation." Catching sight of her hopeful look, he quickly added, "Keep in mind, Mari, that a seduction doesn't work right if you know it's coming. What I'm doing is inviting you to dinner."

"What kind of dinner?"

"Mari, when a man invites you to dinner, you're supposed to act pleased and then accept. You don't ask what he's serving."

By now, Mari knew that he was teasing her. "I'm very pleased and I accept," she said. "Now, what's for dinner?"

Patrick gave an exaggerated sigh. "What am I going to do with you? I'm inviting you to dinner along with an old friend of mine I want you to meet. His name's Fred, and he's in…graphic design."

Actually, Fred had been in car theft and forgery before Patrick took on his rehabilitation. Now he wanted Mari to see that it was possible to change one's life.

"So we won't be alone?"

She sounded so disappointed that he squeezed her hand and reassured her that Fred wouldn't be staying the night. "And before you ask me if you *will* be staying the night, just wait and see. You're wanting far too much information for a potential seductee here."

Mari's smile widened. "I was just wondering if I should bring a toothbrush."

"I have an extra. Now come on. Let's get out of here. It's getting too late to go anywhere else tonight anyway."

Patrick was already heading for the door when Mari said, "Patrick, there's something I have to ask you."

She was chewing on her lip again, and he recognized something serious in her tone.

"Okay," he said carefully, coming back to sit on the edge of the desk. "What is it?"

Mari took a deep breath. "Why were you parked outside my shop the past three nights?"

He was taken aback at the question, because he hadn't thought she had seen him. He pondered the problem of what to tell her. But Mari already had her own theory.

"You got thrown out of your apartment, didn't you?" she asked, her brow furrowed with worry. "It's all right. You can tell me. We can find you something less expensive, or you could even...stay at my place. If you want."

He tried not to smile at both her conclusion and her generosity. "I wasn't thrown out of my apartment," he assured her. "I just left temporarily because of the...new paint."

"Oh." She brightened at that explanation.

"Mari," he said, taking her arm to escort her to the door this time because he had to get up early for work and because if he lingered here with her any longer he was going to forget about the possibility of being struck by lightning if he tried to seduce her in a church. He caught a whiff of her hair, which smelled like flowers and almost made him forget what he was going to say. "Mari, did it ever occur to you that I might be stalking you?"

She looked at him with great surprise as she turned off the last light just before they stepped outside. "No. Why?"

"Because men do that all the time. Some men anyway. You have to be more careful."

"But I'm a really good judge of character," she told him earnestly. "I'm hardly ever wrong about someone."

"You don't say," he said dryly, wondering just what she would say if he confessed his true occupation to her right now. He handed her into her car and leaned on the open window so he could smell her hair again. "By the way, how did you know I was sleeping in my car? Were you watching out your window with binoculars?"

Mari laughed. "Mrs. Kurtz told me. She's head of our local Neighborhood Watch, and she takes her job very seriously. She patrols our block every night."

Here he was, a seasoned detective who'd weathered dozens of stakeouts, and he'd been made by a crusty widow. It only confirmed his suspicion that Mari was spending too much time with senior citizens.

"Come over to my place about six on Friday, okay?" he said, leaning in to kiss her on the cheek. Mari turned slightly, her mouth parted, and Patrick found himself kissing her lips automatically, as if it was what he had wanted to do all along. To his surprise, it was. This little con artist had gotten to him like no other woman, and he found it damn unsettling.

"Are you going to sleep in your car tonight?" she asked softly when he raised his head.

"No, I think the...paint's dry by now," he said, cupping her cheek in his hand. "Go on home and I'll see you Friday."

He stood and watched her car disappear from sight before he walked to his own car. *How could such a sweet little thing get into so much trouble?*

Patrick shook his head and started the engine. Obviously his stakeouts hadn't solved anything. He hadn't managed to catch her doing one thing wrong.

All he had to show for the hot nights sleeping in his car were a stiff neck and wrinkled shirts.

It was time to move on to Phase Two of the Rehabilitation of Mari Lamott. He was determined to make a success of this. She wasn't going to be dodging any more police charges or dancing half-naked on any tables.

Just to make sure, he drove past her shop, relaxing only when he saw her car parked in the alley.

8

Patrick took no chances with dinner. He was a semi-competent cook, but he ordered in pizza because he wanted to be able to give his full attention to the three people coming to dinner. The guest list had increased when Fred told Patrick that he was seeing a woman now, a woman Patrick had once busted for soliciting.

Fred assured Patrick that the woman, Angela, had retired from the trade, and Patrick had believed him. Fred was the world's worst liar, a real liability when he had been a car thief and forger.

Now Patrick was worried, because he wasn't sure that Fred's ineptitude in the lying department wouldn't trip him up when he met Mari. Patrick had stressed to him that he wanted Mari to continue to think that he was a massage therapist and not a cop.

Patrick popped an antacid into his mouth and chewed ferociously. He hadn't touched antacids in years. But, three weeks after meeting Mari, he was eating them like candy.

The doorbell rang, and he opened the door to Fred and Angela, both looking a tad nervous. Patrick was tempted to offer them the antacids.

Angela was a tall, thin brunette with a wide mouth

and nervous eyes. She was clearly uncomfortable, and
Patrick set about putting her at ease. He shook her
hand firmly, smiled and offered her a beer. Her hands
were trembling so much that she nearly dropped it.

Fred and Angela froze as the doorbell sounded
again. This was going to be one long, tense evening,
Patrick thought as he went to answer it. He should
never have put this pair together with Mari.

But he was wrong about that. Mari came in wearing
a little denim jumper with a yellow T-shirt under it,
sandals on her feet and small gold shells on her ears.
She looked good enough to eat, and again Patrick
thought that the evening was going to be a disaster,
but this time it would be because he wouldn't be able
to concentrate on anything but Mari. He intended to
get a head start on that seduction as soon as Fred and
Angela were out the door.

Patrick introduced Fred and Angela as old friends
and let them alone to get the door again, this time for
pizza. When he got back to the kitchen, his three
guests were seated on bar stools at his counter, and
Angela was explaining palm reading to Mari, who
looked up and flushed at his return.

"And this is the Mound of Venus," Angela was
saying. "A prominent one means you're sensible. Like
yours here." Patrick had a feeling the right word was
sensual but he wasn't about to get into a discussion
on palm reading and especially one concerning Mari's
sensuality.

"I hate being sensible," Mari said, sighing. Patrick
nearly dropped the pizza, thinking that sensible was
the last word he would use to describe her.

"Oh, it's a good thing," Angela told her. "I wish

I'd been sensible when I was younger. I wouldn't have ended up in jail.''

"You were in jail?" Mari asked, her eyes wide.

Angela nodded. "Me and Fred both. I was a call girl.''

Mari didn't understand. "You were one of those people who call up during the dinner hour to sell things?''

"Not exactly," Angela said. "I went on dates with men. For money." When Mari still looked blank, she added, "And went to bed with them. Most of the time we didn't even get to the bed though. There was this one guy who got it out right in his car at a stoplight.'' She seemed to realize that she'd gotten a bit too detailed and began studying her nails.

"Oh." Mari turned crimson. "You must know a lot about men.''

Patrick could see right where Mari was headed with that comment. She looked entirely too hopeful that Angela would share more of her experience with the male sex.

Angela sighed. "I should have stayed in school, but I was bored.''

"It's never too late to go back," Mari said, brightening. "I've even tutored a few people who were studying for their General Equivalency Diploma.''

"Really? I can't find a job because everybody wants someone with a diploma. I even thought about going back to turning tricks, but Fred wouldn't let me.''

At this, Fred turned crimson himself, and Patrick opened the antacid bottle again.

"Well, I can't promise anything," Mari said, "but

I know a little restaurant that's looking for a waitress. And I'd be glad to help you study up for the G.E.D.''

Patrick perked right up at the mention of a restaurant. The last thing he needed now was for Mari to get Angela a job dancing nude on tables. His life was complicated enough as it was without riding herd on two women bent on showing off their bodies.

"Mari, I don't know if that's a good idea," Patrick began.

"But Angela needs a job, Patrick. I can take her there tomorrow to apply."

"I'm coming, too," Patrick said with such determination that everybody turned to look at him. "Just to put in a good word," he added.

Patrick opened the pizza then and got Mari a glass of wine.

"Sorry, honey," he murmured to her. "I'm fresh out of Kool-Aid."

That suited Mari just fine. She had been thinking about her Kool-Aid habit and decided that if she was to continue in this exciting, woman-of-the-world vein, she needed to become acquainted with alcohol. And she could use the false courage that wine might give her. She had a feeling that Patrick might spring his seduction on her tonight, and she wanted to be relaxed.

The wine was slightly sweet and tingled her tongue. She quickly drained the first glass and held it out for a refill. Patrick raised his brows but poured.

They ate pizza, listened to old Chuck Berry records and talked. After two beers, Fred told the story of his first car theft and how upset he was when he discovered he was two states away in the mayor's car. He had abandoned it right there and hitchhiked home.

Forgery hadn't gone much better. He had stolen some trash in an upscale neighborhood and rifled through until he found some canceled checks. He practiced the signature until he was sure it was just right, then went to the bank and used a blank check he made out to cash. Unfortunately, the signature he had been practicing so diligently had been that of the bank president, and he ended up in jail.

Mari was giggling by this time, and Patrick couldn't help smiling. He was entertaining the three most inept criminals in the history of the world. Fred and Angela had changed their ways and were law-abiding and happy to be that way. But Mari was...*special*. She was sweet and cute and funny and she really did give a damn about other people instead of paying lip service like so many others did.

He watched her touch Angela's arm while she talked to her, and he felt a warmth in his groin that was more than the beer he was drinking. If he didn't get that promised seduction under way soon, he was going to explode. A rehabilitation and a seduction. He'd certainly undertaken two big projects at once. But another look at Mari's deep brown eyes and he didn't regret either one. If only he could keep her busy enough that she didn't go over to Masonfield to dance nude again.

Fred was talking about a pottery class he and Angela were taking together at the community college starting the following week, and that gave Patrick an idea. He didn't need another project in his life, but Mari did. And learning a hobby would be an excellent step toward her rehabilitation.

"Maybe I'll look into that class myself," Patrick

said, surprised when everyone fell silent and turned to look at him. "What?" he demanded.

Fred cleared his throat. "You just don't seem...I mean, I can't quite picture you..." Patrick could see that Fred was struggling not to call him sergeant in front of Mari.

"Oh, I can," Mari interrupted, beaming. "He has wonderful hands. Long strong fingers. Great pecs. And nice eyes."

Patrick broke in before she could catalog any more of his body parts. "Actually, I can see both of us doing that, Mari. Wouldn't you enjoy a pottery class? Make some cookie jars?"

"Oh, yes," she said with a dreamy look on her face. "Just like that movie I rented last month. The one with Patrick Swayze. He and Demi Moore were sitting at a pottery wheel, and his hands were—"

"We'll sign up for the pottery class," Patrick broke in, knowing exactly where Patrick Swayze's hands were in that movie and what Mari was thinking. Actually, he was thinking the same thing, and he didn't understand why. He had never had so much trouble controlling his libido before. There was definitely something wrong. Stacey had waylaid him on the steps with another of those awful jars of apple butter when he was coming home last night. She had trailed her fingers up his arm, and her mouth was an open invitation. But Patrick had felt no urge to take her to bed, and that had made him think he was losing his mind. The only person he could picture in his bed was a sneaky little con artist whose heart was too soft for her own good.

Actually, women other than Mari were beginning to

annoy him. He had never noticed before that when Stacey was around him she sighed a lot and never quite finished her sentences. And she tended to be more than a little melodramatic when recounting her social life. Not like Mari at all. No, not at all.

Fred and Angela left at midnight, and Patrick smiled as he locked the door after them. Ever since Mari's reference to that movie, all he could think about was getting her into his bed and peeling off her clothes. He wasn't sure even what Fred and Angela had talked about toward the end of the evening. His attention had continued to wander to Mari's face, to that soft mouth and those soulful eyes.

She had been sitting on the couch for the past hour, her feet curled under her, and she had yawned her good-night to their guests. But Patrick had plans that should bring her fully awake. He had even arranged for another detective to cover for him tonight, so there would be no interruption from his pager. He all but rubbed his hands together in anticipation as he turned to her.

And there she was, sleeping soundly on the couch, her head cradled on the padded arm.

Patrick studied her, a smile curving his mouth. He couldn't believe he had once thought her manipulative and unfeeling and out for whatever she could get. She was the most generous woman he knew. And when he had her well rehabilitated and he no longer had to worry about her dancing nude on tables or sitting in jail in her pink feathers, he wanted her to remain his friend. He couldn't imagine the possibility of never seeing her again.

"Come on, friend," he whispered as he bent to pick her up. "Let's get you tucked in for the night."

He put her in his bed, turning the ceiling fan on low and pulling a light blanket over her sleeping form. She made a small sound as she curled into a snail shape, and Patrick felt the now all-too-familiar desire she ignited in him. He was going to have to seduce her soon, he warned himself. For the sake of his sanity if not his physical frustration.

He brought a pillow and another light blanket to the couch, stopping in the bathroom to use the toilet and wash his face. He took one last look at Mari, then got ready to settle down on the couch. Then he decided that he'd better make a note if he and Mari were supposed to pick up Angela and take her to a restaurant tomorrow. He had a feeling that after falling asleep from the wine, Mari might not remember the appointment.

He lay down on the couch, but he knew he couldn't sleep. He pounded the pillow a few times and rolled over, but that didn't work. Neither did a glass of milk. He glanced at the closed bedroom door and made up his mind.

Mari was so sound asleep that she didn't budge when Patrick slipped beside her on the bed. He nudged her a bit with his hip until he had enough room. Then he pulled part of the blanket over his shoulders and put his arm over her waist. Within five minutes he was asleep.

Mari woke up first the next morning, a fuzzy taste on her tongue and a slight pounding in her head. And her body felt like lead. She tried to roll over and couldn't. She pushed harder, then realized that there was a heavy arm resting on her back. She didn't remember Rex having an arm like that, and she craned her head for a better look.

It was Patrick in bed with her. Mari's heart sank— she had slept through the seduction! She didn't remember anything!

Patrick stirred beside her and moved his arm. Mari took advantage of that to sit up. "I'm sorry," she said, and he looked at her in complete bafflement. Her eyes drifted lower, and heat climbed her face when she saw that the cover was twisted around his upper torso, and he wore only boxer shorts.

"You didn't snore, if that's what you're thinking," he said at last.

"But I slept through it." She stole another look at his legs, noting how well muscled they were.

"Slept through what?" He rubbed one eye with the heel of his hand.

"The seduction." She could barely bring herself to say it.

"I see," he said, though it was clear from his voice that he didn't see at all. He took a deep breath and looked around the room as if trying to reorient himself. "Did you seduce me while I was sleeping?"

"No, I thought you seduced me." Her voice trailed off.

"I think I would have remembered something like that," he assured her.

"Then why were we sleeping together?"

"Because you fell asleep on my couch. I was chivalrous enough to give you the bed, but not chivalrous enough to sleep on the couch myself."

"Oh. So nothing happened." She tried to get a better glimpse of his chest, which looked as if it would feel delightfully hard under her hands.

"Not unless you count popping me in the nose. You know, you thrash around an awful lot when you sleep. I finally put my arm over you to hold you still." She was looking at him with such a disappointed expression that he stopped talking and just appreciated how fresh she was for someone who had just awakened. Now that he was awake enough to notice things, he realized that his raging hormones had been awake longer than the rest of him, if certain parts of his anatomy were any indication. "You're a morning person, aren't you?"

She nodded. "Aren't you?"

"Just parts of me, sweetheart." He gave her his best imitation of a lascivious smile, and she grinned back.

"What happens now?" she asked, her eyes glowing.

"First, I get a shower and a cup of coffee," he said, throwing off the cover. "Then...well, you'll just have to wait and see, won't you?"

Her smile broadened. She sat cross-legged in the middle of his bed and watched him with such avid interest that he nearly blushed himself. He found her lack of artifice a refreshing change from the women he'd taken to bed in the past.

Patrick reached the door and cursed suddenly, making Mari jump. "What's wrong?"

"This." He pulled a note from the door and carried it back to the bed, dropping it in front of her.

Mari read it, frowning. *Angela 9:00 a.m.* She looked up at Patrick blankly. "I don't understand."

"We promised Angela we'd take her to that restaurant about a job at nine this morning."

"We did?"

Patrick smiled. "Right before you started on the wine. And we have just enough time to get showered and dressed before we have to pick up Angela." He gave her a significant look. "I'd suggest that we shower together to save time, but I'm afraid we'd end up being...real late. You go ahead, and I'll put on some coffee."

They made it to Angela's apartment more or less on time, Mari still dressed in the denim jumper and T-shirt from the night before. Patrick waited for Mari to give him directions to the restaurant, fully expecting to head toward Masonfield.

But they ended up only two blocks from her shop at a little sandwich place called Bunstead's. The bell on the door tinkled as they entered, and, after one quick look at the lace café curtains and ice-cream parlor tables, Patrick could see that there was no nude dancing here. Four tables were occupied, and a low hum of conversation filled the room.

He got another surprise when Mrs. Kurtz came through a back door that apparently led to a cooler. She had three loaves of bread in her arms, and she brightened the instant she saw them.

"You picked the right day," she assured them. "We've got cinnamon rolls this morning."

Mrs. Kurtz's sister, Leah Hartman—the one whose grandson Patrick had helped—was manning the cash register while Mrs. Kurtz tended the grill, and after the other diners had left, the two sisters took a minute to sit with Mari, Patrick and Angela.

Mari told them that Angela needed a job, delicately refraining from getting specific about her history, but making some veiled references to her "past problems."

The two sisters looked at each other with raised brows and then asked Patrick if those "problems" were similar to those of Leah's grandson, whom Patrick had helped. Patrick assured them that it was definitely the same kind of trouble.

The sisters looked at each other again, then took Angela behind the counter to talk to her alone. Mari turned immediately to Patrick and asked what kind of trouble they were talking about with Mrs. Kurtz and her sister.

"It's confidential," Patrick told her.

"Was it something to do with massages?" she demanded. "It was, wasn't it? Patrick, were you involved in something illegal?"

She looked so worried that he decided he would have to tell her part of the truth anyway. "Mrs. Hartman's grandson, Jack, fell in with a bad crowd a few years ago, and he got involved in some drugs. No crack or meth, but he got caught growing marijuana. I pulled a few strings for him because I thought he was a kid who'd made a mistake."

"You used your connections at the YMCA?" she asked.

"I used my connections, yes," he agreed, unwilling to clarify just what connections those had been.

"Remind me to call you if I ever get in trouble," she said, giving him a pert smile.

Patrick felt his stomach sink to his toes. It suddenly hit him that this was what he had been hoping Mari would do all along, tell him about her troubles and ask for his help. Instead, someone else had bailed her out of jail after the dancing-on-the-tables-in-pink-feathers fiasco. He supposed that wasn't something that a woman would want a less than platonic male friend finding out, but it still bothered him.

"Patrick, I've been a little worried about something," she said, her smile fading.

His heart quickened. "What's that?"

"Well, your friends—Fred and Angela and Mrs. Hartman's grandson. You seem to have more than an average number of friends who've been in trouble with the law. What I've been wondering is...well, have you ever done time?"

"Done time?" he repeated, completely taken aback by her question.

"It's all right, really," she assured him. "I'm an excellent judge of character, and I'm sure it wasn't your fault. I mean, you probably didn't realize what you were getting into, and you did it for a friend, and then you got sent upriver or whatever it is they call it."

Patrick just stared at her. She thought he might be an ex-con! He was all set to be riled over her assumption, but then he decided that at least she didn't suspect the truth.

"I've never been 'upriver' or behind bars or anything else like that," he told her. "I admit that a lot of my friends have been in jail, but they're all straight now. You can count on it. So I wouldn't worry, if I were you."

"Oh, I'm not worried," she said. "I don't have anything against anyone who gets in trouble with the law. I mean, it can happen to anyone, right?''

''But it generally doesn't,'' Patrick said. ''I can accept one mistake in judgment, but there aren't any excuses after that.''

Mari looked so miserable that Patrick realized she must think that she was a lost cause.

''That doesn't mean that someone can't be rehabilitated,'' he said, trying to look stern.

Mari nodded, but she didn't feel any better. Patrick's standards were awfully high, and she was pretty sure that he would be so appalled when he found out about her sister that he wouldn't want anything further to do with her. And a lot of it was Mari's own fault. She should have set more definite limits for her sister, shouldn't have paid her fines and bailed her out of jail. But she still didn't think she could turn a deaf ear if Mariette got into more trouble. She was her sister, after all, and Mari loved her. As much as she wanted Patrick Keegan, she couldn't throw her sister to the sharks—or in this case, the police—just to tidy up her own life.

The problem was, she was falling in love with Patrick, and she didn't know what to do about it. She wasn't nearly as exciting as Patrick thought she was, and she wasn't sure how much longer she could continue to fool him on that count. He would lose interest in her as soon as he found out how plain and ordinary her life really was. And how dull she was, as well.

At least Patrick had interesting friends, even if they were felons.

Angela came bouncing back from the counter with

a wide smile. "I've got a job!" she announced. Mrs. Kurtz and her sister smiled serenely behind her.

They all shared a congratulatory cinnamon roll, then Patrick and Mari took Angela back home. Patrick invited Mari to the game he was coaching that afternoon, and she accepted.

He took the antacid bottle along just in case something else unanticipated cropped up.

Patrick kept one eye on the stands during the game. Davy's grandmother was sitting beside Mari again, but his mother was there, as well, making Patrick hopeful that Mari wouldn't get stuck with any more kittens. Or sign up for any more psychic readings, either.

Davy's friend Andrew was not having a good afternoon, and after striking out three times in a row he began to swear, getting louder with each four-letter word. Patrick sat him on the bench and set about quieting him down. But Andrew was upset over more than his game. His father had just left on a business trip, cancelling a promised outing to an amusement park.

The tragedy of it all got to Andrew, and he began to cry, quietly at first and then with increasing sorrow, repeating, "It's not fair." Patrick looked helplessly toward the stands, feeling as if he were appealing to a Greek chorus. The next instant, he and Andrew were surrounded by Mari, Davy's mother, and his grandmother. Patrick took himself back to the game, glancing worriedly over his shoulder as the women comforted Andrew. He couldn't make himself stop watching Mari as she hugged the boy and finally made him smile with some little comment that Patrick didn't hear.

But whatever it was that she said, Andrew glanced at Patrick, grinned at Mari and nodded his head. Patrick just hoped there wasn't a box of kittens involved in this somewhere.

"So what did you tell him?" Patrick demanded when the game was over and he had stood by congratulating his team members as they left with their parents or grandparents. He fingered the antacid bottle in his pocket.

"Tell who?"

"Andrew. I saw you tell him something that apparently changed his whole outlook." When she didn't immediately answer, he frowned and said, "Well?"

"I told him that you were going to take him out for pizza and then…"

"And then what?" He didn't like the way she was hesitating.

Mari sighed. "I told him you'd give him a massage just like the big leaguers get from their trainers. You will do that, won't you, Patrick?"

Patrick groaned. "Mari, I don't think big leaguers actually get massages from their trainers."

"Well, a rubdown then. I think he really needs a hug, but he can't ask his coach to do that, so this is the next best thing. You'll do it, won't you, Patrick?"

He looked past her at Andrew who was toeing the ground and trying not to look back. It was hard enough to say no to Mari, but Patrick was afraid that if he denied Andrew it would precipitate a whole new string of curses and tears from the boy.

Patrick gave in, but not gracefully. "All right, but I want something in return."

"What's that?" she asked, and he could tell that she was a little worried about what it might be.

"I'll tell you when the time's right," he said.

Mari's eyes widened. "You want me to agree to something when I don't even know what it might be?"

"That's about the size of it," he said, beginning to enjoy the turn the conversation had taken.

"But what if it's something...improper?" she asked.

"Could very well be," he assured her, raising his brows.

"When?" she asked, and he almost laughed. She was never coy, and he was appreciating that trait more and more.

"How about tonight?"

Mari smiled. "You're on."

The pizza outing turned into a crowd scene at the table with Andrew, Davy, and Davy's grandmother joining them, along with Rose whom Mari had insisted they invite. But Mari couldn't concentrate on the conversation or the food. She kept thinking about Patrick and his veiled promise that he would seduce her tonight. Just the prospect made her feel giddy and nervous and incredibly aroused. She managed to eat a slice and a half of pizza, then she sat toying with the crust on her plate and watching Patrick from under lowered lashes.

He was the handsomest man she'd ever met, and the fact that he was going to seduce her—*plain Mari Lamott who knew far more about brownies and pianos than she did about the male sex*—was heady stuff indeed. He had the sexiest smile and the gentlest hands and he was kind to everyone. She couldn't help loving him. But it was a futile love. She had no illusions about that. Once he found out that her life was about as exciting as watching grass grow, he would lose all interest. She supposed that that was inevitable, but she was determined to enjoy what she could now.

For now she was a dashing psychic with a medicine cabinet filled with condoms. And tonight Patrick Keegan was going to seduce her.

Only it didn't quite turn out that way.

Patrick took Rose home and gave Andrew his "training rubdown" there, gently kneading the boy's shoulders and back until he felt the small muscles untense. He got him a glass of milk and two of Rose's cookies and was just about to show Andrew some of the old baseball cards his grandfather had collected when his pager went off. He knew immediately that his plans for Mari had just been canceled.

He was right. A black and white had just pulled over a couple of guys for speeding and found crack sitting right on the front seat. The boys had been out doing some selling, and now they were being questioned about their supplier. Patrick had been working for a month on identifying a local drug supplier, and now he had to go down to talk to them.

Out of earshot of the others, he told Mari that there was a problem with the air-conditioning at the YMCA and he had to go supervise the repair crew. He told her he would call one of his brothers to pick up Andrew and drive him to his aunt's house, then take Mari to his apartment to pick up her car.

Mari walked Patrick outside, her disappointment evident on her face. "Will I see you tomorrow?" she asked.

Patrick would have liked to assure her that she would, but he knew how these cases went. No doubt he would spend tomorrow sweet-talking some judge so he could get a warrant to arrest the supplier. And then there would be the paperwork.

"I don't think so," he admitted, taking her in his arms because she looked so forlorn. "These things have a way of dragging on longer than they should."

Mari nodded. "Maybe I'll take a drive tomorrow then. I've been wanting to check out a new antique shop."

"No!" Patrick said in alarm. "Don't do that."

Mari stared up at him in confusion. "Why not?"

"If I can get away, I will, and I'd hate to come by and miss you," he said, inventing the excuse as he went along. "Maybe we can have some Chinese or something when I get done tomorrow."

Mari smiled. "Okay." She stretched up on tiptoe and whispered in his ear, "Maybe we can have a seduction as well as Chinese."

Patrick smiled and brushed his lips over her cheek. "We'll see."

Mari turned and met his mouth with her own, the taste and feel of his lips instantly heating her. She savored him, thinking that when he finally did seduce her she was going to be more than ready.

"Remember," Patrick said as he pressed one more kiss on her before heading for his car, "don't go anywhere."

As he drove away, Patrick rubbed his neck. He didn't know how he was going to concentrate on questioning the two drug dealers when all he could think about was the worrisome possibility of Mari heading to Masonfield to dance half-naked on a table.

It was going to be a long night.

9

Patrick was so swamped with work that he couldn't get to Mari's apartment on Sunday, and it nearly drove him crazy. He was finally done by midnight, and he drove past the music shop on his way home. There were no lights on, but he noted with relief that her car was parked in the alley.

He fell into an exhausted sleep, waking to the alarm in the morning and groaning as he got ready to go back to work. The first thing he did when he got to the station was call a florist and order some red roses to be delivered to Mari immediately. He hesitated over what to say on the card, then told the clerk, "From Patrick Swayze to Demi Moore."

He called the music shop at noon, feeling immense relief when Mari answered.

"The roses are beautiful," she said, pure happiness in her voice, and it gave him real satisfaction to please her like that. "Did you get the air-conditioning fixed?"

It took him a moment to remember what he had told her. "The air-conditioning. Yeah, sure, it's fine now. Want to grab a bite to eat before the pottery class tonight?"

"I wish I could," she said, sighing, "but I have to give Jimmy Payne a piano lesson."

"How old is this Jimmy Payne?" Patrick asked, and Mari laughed.

"Nine, and he'd rather be playing baseball than playing the piano."

"I'd rather he were playing baseball, too," Patrick assured her. "How about if I pick you up to go to the class?"

"Okay. I'll see you then."

Patrick had expected a small class of less than ten people. He figured that he wouldn't know anyone other than Fred and Angela, and that suited him just fine. It would give him a chance to have some time with Mari.

So when they walked in and he saw Mrs. Kurtz and her sister, Leah, along with Davy's grandmother and his own grandmother, all milling around the registration table, he was more than a little taken aback. "What are you doing here?" he demanded of Rose, a little more testily than he intended, after Mari had moved on ahead of him to register.

"The class sounded like fun, dear," she said.

"So you recruited half the town to come along?" He continued to scowl at her.

"Well, I thought that you and Mari might like a little company."

"Company?" His brows went up. He was beginning to understand this sudden interest of his grandmother and her friends in pottery. They were chaperoning him and Mari. "Listen," he said, "I'm not going to romance Mari and then throw her in jail, if that's what you're thinking. I'm just going to rehabilitate her.''

"Is that what you call it?'' Rose asked mildly.

"Dammit, Gram, she's a con artist.''

"I don't believe I ever saw any money change hands,'' Rose reminded him archly.

"All right, she's the world's worst con artist. And...'' He paused significantly, raised his brows and lowered his voice even more. "She sometimes dances on tables in nothing but pink feathers.''

Rose rolled her eyes. "Pink feathers are better than nothing. Or are you going to try to convince me that she stole the feathers?''

Patrick could see that this was a losing battle. His grandmother and her cronies were determined to protect Mari—from him, of all things!

"I'm only trying to set her straight,'' he told Rose more calmly. "I'm not going to hurt her.''

Rose pointed one gnarled finger at him. "You'd better not, or you'll have a lot of people to answer to, Patrick.''

He had a vision of himself surrounded by cane-wielding seniors, but he couldn't dwell on it because the pottery teacher, a heavyset woman wearing beads, was heading toward him, smiling, a registration form in her hands.

Patrick filled out the form, paid his money, and tried to pay attention to the class. The teacher had seated them at a large, round table and was going over the process involved in making pottery, from digging the clay to firing and glazing the finished product. He hoped he wasn't going to be required to dig clay, because he was having enough trouble staying tuned in to what the woman was saying. Mrs. Kurtz and Leah had stationed themselves on either side of him, effectively keeping Mari from sitting with him, and he was pretty annoyed. Fred kept shooting him sympathetic glances, but Patrick barely noticed. He was straining to hear what Mari was saying to Angela.

Angela laughed, and Patrick leaned back farther to see around Leah.

"He's one of a kind," Mari was saying. "Beautiful green eyes and the most darling nose."

Patrick unconsciously touched his nose. He had never thought of it as *darling*.

"And when he climbs into my lap, I just melt."

Climbs into her lap! Just how had she gotten so intimate so fast with someone new? He thought he was keeping her so busy that she had no time to get herself into trouble, either with the law or with some other man. And here she was, talking about someone climbing into her lap.

Patrick opened his mouth to demand an explanation of her newfound sweetie, when Angela asked, "Where should I put the litter box?"

Litter box?

Patrick quickly closed his mouth, realizing now that Mari was apparently giving one of the kittens to Angela. What was wrong with him? When he had thought that she was talking about a new man in her life, he had felt his stomach turn sickeningly. It must be the milk shake he'd gulped down on his way to pick up Mari. He looked across the table and found his grandmother eyeing him disapprovingly. He popped an antacid into his mouth and tried to concentrate again on the teacher.

The class was interminable. They shaped clay into coils and spirals and circles and balls. By the end of the evening, Patrick was ready to force feed the clay to the teacher. He was tired of this whole business. And he wanted to be alone with Mari.

Not that he needed Mari. It was just that he had promised her a seduction, and he was growing weary of everyone else getting in the way.

Rose tried to interest Mari into going for a cup of coffee after the class ended, but Patrick was having none of that.

"I'm taking Mari home," he told her, glancing darkly around at everyone else in case one of them dared to press the invitation. "She has plenty of coffee there."

Eyebrows went up at his tone, but no one said a word.

Patrick was still fuming when he followed Mari upstairs to her apartment. The first thing he did was go to the bathroom and wash his hands to get that damn clay off his skin. His quiet evening keeping Mari out of trouble had turned into something else entirely.

When he came back out, Mari was bending to stroke the lone kitten, which arched its back to her touch as it nibbled at the cat food in the dish. Rex sat on the counter beside the vase of red roses, watching the whole operation with disdain.

"Where are the other two?" Patrick asked.

Mari grinned at him. "I gave them away already. Davy took one and Jimmy Payne the other. Angela wants this one." She sank onto the couch and stretched out her legs. "My shoulders ache from punching that clay all night."

Patrick moved behind her and automatically began to knead her shoulders, still frowning. "I can't believe the Gray Panthers decided to join the pottery class," he complained.

"I thought it was fun," Mari said. "Mrs. Kurtz is planning on making a vase for every table in the coffee shop."

"Mrs. Kurtz should make herself a helmet and take up skydiving," he said irritably. "Something she can do alone."

"Mmm, that feels good," Mari said, pulling her legs onto the couch and lowering herself to her stomach. "Could you do my back, Patrick? It aches right between the shoulder blades."

Patrick came around the couch and sat, moving his hands to her back. He rubbed her automatically, his mind still on that damn pottery class. He should have signed them both up for something more useful, a cooking class or gardening. But Mari could cook exceptionally well, and he could find no fault with the flower beds in her backyard.

He had only wanted to keep her busy anyway, to keep her out of trouble. She still visited the nursing home every Wednesday night, and sometimes on Thursday evenings she did volunteer work at the library, shelving books. Fridays, Saturdays and Sundays, Patrick could come up with enough things to keep her occupied between dinner out and a movie. And now the pottery class was on Mondays. So all he really had to worry about was Tuesday evening. He was thinking that maybe he could come up with something for them to do that night. Maybe he would take her square dancing again. He had enjoyed the way her eyes sparkled as she was do-si-do-ing around the floor.

"This is a very good massage, Patrick," Mari said, stretching out her arms. "I bet you have dozens of clients."

"Never an idle moment," he rejoined, frowning. He was going to have to tell her the truth at some point, but he was reluctant to do it yet. He knew that she wasn't a hardened criminal by any means. She was far too kind and softhearted for that. She had probably just been misguided, a little wild in her youth, looking for thrills. But now that she'd met Fred and Angela and seen that a person could live a perfectly nice life without conning widows and dancing on tabletops, and now that she had other things to do with her nights, he was sure that she would settle down.

"It's a little warm in here," Mari murmured. She raised herself enough to tug off the oversize cotton blouse she was wearing, revealing a little pink stretch tank top underneath.

Patrick barely noticed. He was still frowning, his eyes looking at Mari but not seeing as he mentally planned more activities to keep her occupied. Tomorrow he would recommend Mari as a music teacher to every parent on the force.

"It feels warm in here," Mari said softly, turning over on her back and unfastening her jeans. Patrick went on methodically rubbing her shoulders from the front now as he mentally counted the number of officers who had kids.

To his surprise, Mari suddenly sat up, and when he looked at her face he saw tears in her eyes and a trembling lip. Her jeans were halfway down her thighs, but she didn't seem to notice.

"What's wrong, honey?" he asked at once, concerned.

"I must be the least sexy woman on the face of the earth," she whispered, struggling not to let the tears fall. She crossed her arms over her chest, and, for the first time, Patrick noticed how softly rounded her breasts were in the stretch top. "Even Warren G. Harding told me I was plain and uninteresting," she said on a ragged sigh that threatened tears again. "'Like a baked potato with no butter or sour cream,' were his exact words." Her lip trembled some more, and this time a tear slipped from her eye.

"Sweetheart, Warren G. Harding is an idiot," he said gently, confused and worried about her sudden change of mood.

"Then why can't I do it right?"

"Do what right?" he asked, totally confused now.

"Seduce you." The last word was uttered on a soft sob, and the next thing Patrick knew, she had buried her face in her hands and was softly crying.

Patrick felt like a complete and callous fool. She had been trying to seduce him, and he'd been so caught up in planning her rehabilitation that he hadn't even noticed. The fact that her feelings were hurt made him so angry with himself that he would have punched himself in the nose if he had a spare set of hands.

But he didn't. And his hands were currently involved in stroking back Mari's hair and framing her face.

Her legs were stuck out stiffly in front of her, hobbled by the jeans, and Patrick carefully pulled them off after removing her shoes. One good look at that pink tank top and those little white panties, and Patrick was immediately aroused, all thoughts of Mari's rehabilitation gone.

Mari hiccuped and wiped one hand over her eyes. "It's a pretty sad state when a girl tries to seduce a man in this day and age and he doesn't even know it."

"I may not have known what you were doing, honey," Patrick said gently, "but that doesn't mean you weren't doing a good job of it." To prove his point, he adjusted himself, and Mari's eyes widened.

"But you didn't seem interested in the least," she protested.

"That's the thing about men," he told her. "The mind may be occupied elsewhere, but the body generally notices a seduction all on its own." Her feet were curled under her now, and she was pressed against the side of the couch. Patrick saw that he was going to have to coax her back into the mood.

"What were you going to do next?" he asked, raising his brows hopefully.

"I was going to kick off my shoes and then my jeans."

"And after that?" he prompted her.

"Well, by then I was hoping that you'd be a little more…involved in the whole thing."

"Oh, I'm involved right now," he assured her, reaching out to catch the straps of her tank top and lower them until the pale swell of her breasts came into view.

"Would you take something off for me?" she whispered.

"That's what I'm doing, honey."

"No, I mean take something of *yours* off." When he hesitated, she added, "Warren looked like a big tuna with his clothes off and you...don't."

"Let's leave old Warren G. out of this tonight," Patrick said, tugging his shirt over his head. "I don't like to think about fish while I'm seducing a lady."

Mari smiled with delight. Patrick's chest was solid and sprinkled with curly blond hair that angled down toward the top of his jeans and beyond. "What should I do now?" she asked.

"You, sweetheart, should do whatever you feel like doing. Let your instincts take over." To help her along, he leaned over and began to nibble lightly on her neck. He smiled as her breathing quickened audibly. Her arms went around his neck, and she squirmed against him.

Patrick's own need was growing, but he wanted this seduction to be for her alone. He moved his lips to the tender, plump flesh at the top of her breasts and began to play there, tasting and teasing. When she was breathing even harder, he leaned back long enough to lift the tank top over her head and toss it on the floor. Her breasts were beautiful, pale and soft and tipped with peach-colored nipples that were hard.

Patrick stroked her breasts with his fingers first, circling, then lightly pinching the nipples, then stroking around them again until Mari was moaning. She felt as if she were drowning in thick air, but she liked the feeling. Her body felt leaden with pleasure, and there was a growing warmth deep inside her. She murmured his name, then reached out to unbuckle his belt.

"What should I do?" she asked softly, her hands feathering down his hips as she pushed his jeans down.

"Just what you're doing," he whispered, helping her by lifting up and then dropping his shoes and jeans onto the floor with her tank top. Now they both sat on the couch in only underpants—his boxers, her scrap of silk. With any other woman he would have felt silly, but it was just natural with Mari. He pulled her to him, then turned her around and cradled her on his lap. In this position, he could continue to play with her breasts while he went back to nibbling on her neck.

Mari shivered with pleasure. She had willed herself not to think about what would happen after tonight or whenever Patrick found out that she was not only not a psychic, but her life was so dull an authorized biography would barely make a want ad. Tonight she was still the exciting Mari, the woman who lived on the edge—or at least within hollering distance of the edge. And the pleasure that Patrick was giving her now was so sweet and beguiling that she couldn't get enough.

"Oh," she whimpered softly as his exploring fingers caressed lower until they edged beneath the lace of her panties. The heat in her body was becoming like flame, most of it concentrated right where his insistent fingers played. Her breathing was even more ragged, and she pressed herself back against him.

"I want to touch you," she managed to say.

"I think it's time for the seduction to move to the bedroom." He stood and picked her up, cradling her against his naked chest. She was entranced with his hard jaw, caressing it with her fingertips as he carried her. She wanted to memorize every moment of this. Her memory of tonight would be her sweetest treasure when she had to go back to being plain, dull Mari Lamott. At least she would have the satisfaction of knowing that she had loved a man, and he had made love to her.

Patrick set her on the bed, raising his brows only slightly at the two teddy bears who shared the pillow. He left her momentarily to turn on the small lamp by the bedside, then stripped down the comforter, rolling her to one side to accomplish the unmaking of the bed she had so neatly made that morning.

"Sorry, fellows," he said, setting the teddy bears onto a nearby chair. "The lady's all mine tonight."

When Mari was lying on the pillows in nothing but her wispy underpants, the bedside light glowing on her pale skin, her hair in disarray on the pillow, Patrick smiled in satisfaction.

"Lovely," he said. "Now I just need one other little thing. Do you still have that wine?"

Mari nodded. "Could I have mine over ice?"

Patrick's smile broadened. "That's an excellent idea."

Mari had thought that they would drink the wine. But it turned out that Patrick had other ideas. He returned with two glasses of white wine, an ice cube in one, then set about showing her how to use wine creatively in a seduction.

"Take a sip," he told her softly, holding the glass with ice to her lips. Mari drank, feeling only heat as the wine went down her throat. Then, his eyes holding hers, Patrick dipped his fingers into the glass and trailed wine down her chest and between her breasts. Mari gasped as the cool liquid settled into the valley there. His eyes still on her, Patrick lowered his head, and his lips followed the trail, very slowly and very carefully licking it.

Mari squirmed and whimpered softly.

Patrick continued this treatment on every sensitive and intimate place he could find. He trickled it over her arms, down her legs and in her navel. He licked, kissed and caressed until she thought she couldn't stand it any longer.

Patrick was becoming more aroused than he could remember just watching her reactions, but he was determined to add one more refinement to their love play before he took her.

His own breathing was becoming as ragged as hers and his eyes as fever-bright with passion as he slipped the ice cube from her glass and began to touch her here and there with it, to trail it over her heated flesh, then kiss and bite where it touched.

Mari was nearly mindless now. She hadn't imagined that this…this sweet torment, was what lovemaking was like. It had been sweaty and awkward and less than pleasurable with Warren, but now she felt as if she'd stumbled into heaven. Every nerve sang with need, and each place Patrick touched sparked fire. But it was a fire that flared more hotly with each stroke of ice and tongue.

"I'll be right back," he murmured, making her chew her lip with anxiety as he left the bedroom. He was back a moment later with his wallet, cursing sharply as he opened it.

"What's wrong?" she asked.

Patrick sat on the edge of the bed and touched her hair gently. "I don't have any protection with me."

"Protection?"

"Condoms, honey."

"Oh! Well, I do."

He watched in surprise as she hurried to the bathroom and returned a minute later with an array of boxes balanced on a glass makeup tray.

Patrick tried not to laugh, but he couldn't help himself.

"Mari," he said, pulling her down on the bed with her booty, "that's the strangest dessert tray I've ever seen."

He thumbed through her selections, raising his brows at the flavored condoms, and took a plain one. He had his shorts off and the condom on in an instant, with Mari watching intently.

"Now, where were we?" he whispered, grinning.

Patrick lay beside her, stroking her lips with wine-soaked fingers until she greedily lapped at them with her tongue. She rolled onto her side and eagerly began exploring him with fingertips and mouth. With a sly smile, she took the melting ice cube from his hand and slid it into her mouth. Then she continued her exploration, sometimes letting the ice touch his skin and sometimes only her cool lips.

Patrick couldn't take much more of this, but she was enjoying the play so much that he gripped the sheets and held back the impulse to roll her onto her back and enter her right that moment.

"Enough," he finally groaned when she slid down to the end of the bed and wreaked more havoc on his senses.

"I never saw a man...completely naked before," she whispered playfully while she stroked him where he throbbed.

"I thought you and Warren—"

She nodded her head quickly, then said, "He wanted all the lights out before he'd even take off his vest." She smiled devilishly as she bent her mouth to Patrick. "Now that I think about it, maybe he didn't have a knee fetish so much as he just couldn't tell what was what in the dark."

Patrick started to laugh, but it turned into a groan as she kissed and caressed him. He couldn't wait any longer. Taking hold of her arms, he slid her up and over him. Her legs were spread, straddling him, and now he took one hand and began to stroke her upper thighs and then higher.

Heat spiraled through Mari again, as swift as a flash fire. Her breath came out in a pant. She felt vulnerable and exposed, but the excitement was maddening as his intimate caresses drove her to the brink.

Then he was inside her, urging her down on top of him. Mari was trembling from the tension in her body, from the need that seemed to grow by the moment. It was pleasure and a driving desire so strong that it overwhelmed everything else she had ever known. Without any conscious volition, she began to move on him, hearing his voice spurring her on.

The heat and scent of their bodies enveloped her, made her strong and weak at the same time. The pleasure was mounting, and she whimpered his name.

"Yes, honey," he groaned. "Yes, Mari."

And that was what sent her over the edge, the sound of her name on his lips.

She drifted off to sleep, more content than she could ever remember, and woke later with Patrick's arm over her waist. She turned slightly and studied him in the dim light from the lamp that was still on. His eyes opened slowly, and then he smiled.

"You know, Mari, I didn't realize that you were so good at seduction." His voice was husky with sleep and with a passion that still wasn't quenched.

"I was...okay then?" she asked hesitantly.

Patrick tried not to smile. "Do you want me to fill out my standard evaluation form?" he asked, and she swatted his arm.

"Mari," he said, cupping her chin and turning her to look at him, "first, understand that you are wonderful. Second, the man could always use a little praise himself for his delicate ego." He touched a finger to her lips when she would have said something. "And third, did I mention that you're wonderful?"

She grinned at him and sat up, beginning to run her fingers down his chest. "You weren't so bad yourself," she said.

"That's all my ego gets?" he asked with mock disappointment.

She nodded, devilment in her eyes. "You've got to work for anything more."

Mari pulled back the sheet and began to kiss his stomach.

"Well, if you're sure there's no other way," he said, his voice thickening just before he pulled her up for a hard kiss.

10

Patrick went with Mari to deliver flowers and some fruit to the hospital on Tuesday night. Someone from Mari's church had had her gallbladder removed, and Mari was apparently the only member of the Sunshine Committee who had enough time for the duty—actually, the chore, Patrick decided after he listened to the woman give the gory details for the third time that evening.

Wednesday night he went to the Sunset Acres Rest Home with her while she played piano for a roomful of churlish residents who lapsed into an argument about who got the most applesauce for dinner during Mari's playing of "Blue Moon." But, even that didn't discourage Mari. All the way home she went on about how exciting it was to see the woman with the cane say more than five words at a time.

"Mari, she threatened to take out her teeth and throw them at that man she claimed is the cook's favorite." Patrick took her arm and patiently led her upstairs to her apartment.

"But she never used to get excited about anything, Patrick," she protested. "She's getting involved in things again." She flipped on the kitchen light and busied herself at the sink, opening a can of cat food for Rex.

Patrick leaned against the counter and watched her. It was only a matter of time before some other needy seniors' group latched on to her. He was surprised that the American Association of Retired Persons wasn't camped on her doorstep, recruiting her for a letter-stuffing campaign. If she wasn't careful, she was going to find herself giving away another box of kittens. And she wasn't careful. She cared too much about people to watch out for her own interests.

He sighed and began rearranging the magnets on her refrigerator. What she needed was a vacation. It was something he could use, as well, and the magnets gave him an idea.

"Have you been to Chicago often?" he asked, moving the skyscraper magnet to the side.

"Chicago?" she asked. "I've never—" She broke off when she saw the magnet. "Oh. Chicago. Yes, lots of times." She chewed her lip. "Why?"

"I thought you might like to go there this weekend."

"To Chicago?"

"Sure. We can catch the train Friday night and come back home on Sunday."

"You're asking me to go away for the weekend with you?"

"I'm pretty sure that's what I just said."

Mari had never had such an invitation before, and she wasn't certain what the proper response should be. Or what she should pack. There must be some protocol to this going away with a man for the weekend, but she had no idea what it was. And the matter of finances was tricky. Since she had spent her vacation money bailing Mariette out of jail, she didn't have enough left for a trip to Chicago.

"I—I can't afford it right now, Patrick. Maybe we could do something else instead."

So that was it, Patrick thought. She didn't have enough money. That explained a lot. Like why she felt compelled to dance half-naked on tables.

"Don't worry about money," he said. "I'll take care of it."

"Oh, I couldn't let you do that," she said. "It wouldn't be right. Maybe I can...come up with some money by the weekend." She didn't like to borrow money, and she was generally opposed to using credit cards. But maybe just this once she could charge the trip.

"No!" Patrick said, getting a sudden vision of Mari naked but for pink feathers, gyrating on a table, with men throwing money at her. "I'll pay for the trip."

"But, Patrick—"

He searched his mind for a way to prevail in this. "Remember when you asked me to give Andrew a massage and I told you that I wanted something in return?" he asked.

"Well, yes."

"This is what I want. I want you to come to Chicago with me and to let me pay for everything."

Mari shrugged her shoulders helplessly. This went against her grain.

"Well, all right," she said, frowning.

Patrick moved closer to her and began to rub her shoulders. "What's wrong, honey? Don't you want to spend the weekend with me?"

"Yes. Oh, yes. It's just that I feel funny about you paying my way."

Patrick gave a low laugh. "You're one of a kind. You're the only woman I know who would object on those grounds."

"I am?" She turned her head to study his face.

"You are," he assured her, brushing his lips over her cheek. "And you know what? After Chicago, I think we'll plan to visit every one of those places you have there on your refrigerator, magnet by magnet. And you can be my tour guide. I've never been to the east coast." He nodded toward the crab magnet that said Baltimore. "I'm going to become as much a traveler as you are."

"That sounds…exciting," she said weakly. How was she ever going to tell him that not only had she never been to Baltimore, she'd never even been out of state?

"Maybe we could get an early start," he suggested. "I think I can get a couple of days off. How about you? Want to leave tomorrow instead?"

Mari was chewing on her lip. "I promised Angela I'd help her study for her G.E.D. tomorrow night. We're going to go to your grandmother's house."

"Gram's? How come?"

"Rose is interested in becoming a G.E.D. tutor herself."

"My grandmother?" he asked in surprise. "How come I haven't heard about this?"

"You probably weren't listening," Mari said tartly, squealing when he gave her a playful swat on the behind.

"Do you know how much you've turned my life

upside down?'' he asked with mock dismay, turning her in his arms. ''When I met you at my grandmother's I thought you were a money-grubbing little cheat with too much ambition for her own good.''

''You did?'' Her eyes widened.

''Of course I did. And even though I thought you were pretty cute—''

''You think I'm cute?'' she asked happily.

''More than that, sweetheart. You're someone who embraces life wholeheartedly, who grabs for the brass ring.''

Mari tried to smile, but she couldn't. That wasn't her at all. That was the Mari Lamott she'd tried to be for Patrick. That was a dream woman spun out of lies and an ad for a psychic.

''Of course there are certain things you're going to have to tone down a bit,'' he warned, amusement in his eyes.

''And what would those be?'' She was desperately hoping he would say that he didn't want her to be quite so exciting or well traveled or…impulsive.

''You're a natural sucker for anyone with gray hair and dentures. And, frankly, I don't like having to share you with every Tom, Dick and Harriet who's drawing social security.''

Mari sighed. ''I like older people, Patrick.''

''I know you do,'' he said, more gently now. ''Which is probably a good thing, because one of these days I'm going to be older myself.'' He raised his brows, and she managed to laugh at that. ''But for now I could use some more practice with that seducing business. I'm not sure we got it exactly right.''

"This time," she said, setting aside her anxiety, "I get the ice cube."

"You bet you do," he said with a slow smile.

Patrick sat in the chair staring blankly out the window as he listened to Mari's voice. She was going over presidents with Angela, and they'd been at it for an hour now. Rose had sat in on the first half hour, but her knees had begun to bother her so she'd moved to the porch, standing now and then to walk a bit. Patrick liked listening to Mari's voice, so instead of moving out onto the porch with his grandmother, he sat where he was. He couldn't help but smile when the two got to Warren G. Harding. He glanced over at Mari, but she wouldn't look at him. Still, he could see her blushing, and that made his smile widen.

"My head's overflowing with presidents," Angela complained wearily. "Let's take a break."

"Okay," Mari said. "I could use some more lemonade anyway."

"There are cookies on the counter," Rose called from the porch.

"I'll get them," Patrick offered, lightly squeezing Mari's shoulder as he passed her. "Angela, do you want some more lemonade, too?"

"Thanks." She leaned back in her chair and massaged her neck. "So what are you doing this weekend?"

Mari hesitated before answering. "Actually, Patrick and I were thinking of going out of town."

"Really? Where?"

"Chicago."

Angela sighed. "I wish I could get back there for a

couple of days. I used to live there. Had a job in a department store. Well, for a while anyway." She smiled ruefully. "I took a couple of things home to try on. Without ringing them up, if you know what I mean. End of job."

Mari made a sympathetic sound.

"You know, I never stuck with anything in my life. Least not after the fun wore off. But I promised myself I was going to get my high school diploma, no matter what."

"And I'm holding you to that promise," Mari said. "So are you doing anything this weekend?"

"Fred and I are going to go to the county fair. They've got a country music show on Saturday night." Angela patted her stomach. "And they've got the best funnel cakes and the biggest Ferris wheel."

Mari rested her chin on her hand. "How high does the Ferris wheel go?"

Angela shrugged. "Not sure. But you can see the whole fairgrounds from the top. I love to sit up there with Fred and watch the lights."

"Does it play music, too?" Mari asked.

"Haven't you ever ridden a Ferris wheel?" Angela asked.

"Well...no," Mari admitted.

"You're kidding me! Why not? Were you afraid of them?"

"I guess I never went anywhere that had one," Mari said matter-of-factly. "My grandmother lived with us, and she didn't get out much."

Patrick set the lemonade glasses on the table and went back to the kitchen for the cookies. When he returned, Mari and Angela were talking about presidents again, and Patrick slipped out the door to the porch.

He couldn't believe that Mari, with all of her travel experience, had never ridden a Ferris wheel. Well, he intended to remedy that.

"How are your knees feeling?" he asked Rose, sitting on the top step while she paced with her cane behind him.

"It's going to rain," she told him. "And they're not so bad considering they're eighty years old. Show me a car that can run that long."

Patrick smiled. "And they can predict the weather to boot."

Rose lowered herself slowly into the wicker chair by the railing. "Do you remember Leah Hartman's grandson, the one you helped when he got into trouble?"

"How could I forget?" he asked lightly. "Every Christmas the guy sends me a fruit basket, cheese, fruitcake, and a family photo. He's got two little girls now."

"He's grateful for what you did," Rose said. "I guess you also remember that young man who was a friend of his, the one who got into that drunk driving accident?"

"He's made quite a name for himself in the police ledgers," Patrick said dryly. "He lost his license for a while, but it hasn't slowed him down yet."

"I ran into his aunt in the grocery store the other day, and it seems he's in trouble again. A hit-and-run."

Patrick grunted noncommittally. He had read the report.

"His blood-alcohol level was over the legal limit, but Marilyn—that's his aunt—says he just had a couple of beers."

Patrick snorted. "That's what they all say."

Rose sighed. "Well, the point is that Marilyn asked me if you could do anything to help."

"The help he needs is in a treatment program," Patrick said shortly. "He's been sentenced to two of them so far, but it hasn't done any good. I can't picture the judge giving him anything but jail time now. And I'm certainly not going to do anything to change the judge's mind."

"I know," Rose said, sighing again. "You're right. He's gotten away with too much already. His whole family made excuses for him so long that he thinks it's his right to do whatever he wants without consequences. I feel sorry for him, actually."

"I feel sorry for the next person he runs over while he's drunk," Patrick said sharply, narrowing his eyes to look out at the street. "He's had enough chances to change. It's time he started paying the price."

Inside the house, Mari turned away from the door with a worried frown. She didn't know why a massage therapist from the YMCA had influence in police cases, but it was Patrick's unforgiving tone that had her chewing her lip. For a long time now she had wanted to tell him about Mariette, but she had worried about how he would react to the sudden disclosure of a sister with a police record.

His reaction seemed even more predictable now and not very pleasant.

Angela came out of the bathroom and stretched before sitting back down at the dining room table. "You ready to hit the presidents again?" she asked.

"Sure," Mari said. But her mind was still on Patrick's words. *It's time he started paying the price.*

Mari had a sinking feeling that there was another price to be paid, and it would fall to her to pay it for letting Patrick believe that she was someone she wasn't.

Sitting on the porch with Patrick, Rose and Angela after the tutoring session was done, Mari felt an ache so keen that she had to take a deep breath. All the while she was growing up, this was what she had wanted, to be surrounded by family and friends and to be loved. Here was everything she had yearned for, right here on this porch.

She knew that Patrick liked her, and he certainly enjoyed her in bed. And she thought that he might even be in love with her. But what he loved was all an illusion. Once she told him about Mariette and how dull her own life was, he would realize that he'd made a mistake.

Mari tilted her head back and scanned the night sky. The stars were especially clear tonight with not a cloud to dim them. Warm air hugged her, and the soft sound of crickets and frogs chorused around her. Next to her on the step, Patrick reached over and took her hand in his. It was so perfect that she almost started crying.

Mariette had always gotten what she wanted when she and Mari were children. If she didn't, she either pitched a fit or ran away. Mari, on the other hand, learned to defer her own wants, first to appease her alcoholic mother and then to ease the strain on her grandmother who was too old and too unaccustomed to turmoil to cope with both an alcoholic daughter and a hellcat of a granddaughter. Mari was the peacemaker and the solver of problems. It was her unspoken duty to make everything all right for everyone.

She was tired of that now. For once she wanted things to be all right for her. She wanted the love that she had given to her mother and her sister and her grandmother to finally be returned to her by a man. By Patrick.

He squeezed her hand, and Mari bit back the tears. She wished she had never let him believe that she was someone she wasn't. Then she would never have known how much she was going to miss him.

Mari was normally an efficient packer, but on Friday afternoon the suitcase lay only half filled on her bed. She couldn't decide what to take. She wanted to look attractive but not flashy. Her heart had ruled her head again, and she had decided not to tell Patrick the truth yet about herself or Mariette. She wanted to have a memorable, romantic weekend with him before the ax fell.

Rex wandered into the bedroom and jumped up onto her dresser to watch the proceedings. It had rained most of the morning, and he was restless.

"Weekend away with a man," Mari informed him archly. "My first and probably my last." She threw a long black skirt into the suitcase and was about to hunt for a blouse when the phone rang.

It was Mariette, and Mari's heart sank. She sat on the bed and ran a hand through her hair.

"You've got to help me, Mari," Mariette pleaded. "It wasn't my fault. Really."

"It never is, is it?" Mari returned wearily. "What happened now?"

"Harmon and I needed gas for the Harley—did I tell you we're going away for the weekend? Anyway, we didn't have any money, and I didn't think it would hurt to just put a couple of bucks in and drive off. It wasn't like I was stealing. I was going to pay the station back once I got a job."

"I'm afraid it *is* stealing," Mari said sharply.

"Mari, I know you said I was on my own after last time, but they're going to put me in *jail* for good this time! These Masonfield police aren't kidding."

Mari could hear the tears in Mariette's voice, and she rubbed her forehead with her fingers. She felt tears welling in her own eyes. She knew what she was going to do. She might have told Mariette that she was on her own now, but the reality proved a lot more difficult. Mari had played the keeper and caretaker for so long that she couldn't escape the feelings of responsibility. She couldn't make herself turn her back on her sister.

"All right. I'll be there as soon as I can."

"Harlon will be waiting for you."

She hung up feeling years older than before she'd answered the phone. She supposed that when it came right down to it, she couldn't really change herself. She could pretend that she was exciting, impulsive and carefree until the cows came home, but she would never really believe it inside.

Her fingers trembled as she dialed Patrick's number.

"Something's come up, Patrick," she said quietly when he answered. "I'm afraid I can't go to Chicago with you."

"What is it?" he asked with obvious concern. "What's wrong?"

"It's nothing I can't deal with," she said carefully. "I'm sorry about this. I really am."

"Mari, this doesn't make sense. If you don't want to go, just say so. I know you were hesitant about the trip."

"I'm not making excuses, Patrick," she said, impatience warring with sadness. "I have to go somewhere else."

"Tell me where, then. Mari, we were planning to go away together for the weekend. A person doesn't just cancel that without a damn good reason."

Oh, she had a damn good reason all right. She just couldn't share it with him. *Well, if you must know, my sister's in jail again. And while you're absorbing that shock, let me add that she's the exciting one in the family. I spend all my time cleaning up her messes because I have nothing better to do with my life.*

"I'm sorry, Patrick," she repeated. "But I can't give you the reason."

"For once, Mari, why don't you just be honest with me?" he demanded, his patience at a sudden end. Patrick hadn't meant to press her, especially after hearing her voice catch, but he was tired of her evasiveness. She should know by now that he cared about her and what happened to her. She should know that she could trust him. Instead, she was still hiding things from him.

Mari swallowed hard with anxiety. Surely he hadn't guessed that her image was all a lie, a carefully constructed front.

"I don't know what you mean," she said, but she didn't sound convincing even to her own ears.

"Don't you think I know about the trips to Masonfield? I'm not stupid."

"You know?" she repeated stupidly.

"Did you really think I'd never find out? How long were you going to try to keep it a secret?" His anger was building as he thought about how deceitful she had been, how she hadn't trusted him enough even after they slept together.

"I didn't think—" she began, but he cut her off.

"No, you didn't think."

Mari didn't know what to say. There didn't seem any way to patch things up now that he'd found out on his own. It would have been bad enough if she had just told him herself, but at least then she would have had the satisfaction of knowing she'd done the right thing. But now...

Patrick finally broke the silence. "Do you want to talk about it?"

She did, desperately, but she couldn't—not now.

"I can't," she said in misery. "Not right now."

"Then maybe we don't have anything to talk about at all."

"Patrick!" She bit back tears. "I'm sorry." She hung up the phone before she could change her mind. Grabbing her purse, she all but ran out the door. And she cried the entire drive to Masonfield. She'd lost Patrick. But she'd never really had him in the first place. It was the exciting Mari he liked, the one who didn't come encumbered with lies and a semiprofessional criminal sister.

* * *

Harlon was waiting for her at the police department, pacing in front of the door. A short, red-haired sergeant at the desk did a double take when Mari walked in. A chair in one corner was filled with an older man in a trenchcoat who was obviously inebriated. He looked at Mari with interest.

"All right," Mari said without any preliminaries. "What's the deal this time?"

"She needs a lawyer," Harlon told her, looking sheepish. "And we can't pay for one."

"That's what public defenders are for," Mari said sharply, feeling far less sympathetic toward Mariette since her conversation with Patrick. She had just lost the man she loved, and a great deal of the blame lay at Mariette's door. Mari's one great love affair hadn't lasted quite a month.

"You've got to help us," Harlon pleaded. "My family won't. I already tried them. And you're all Mariette's got. I don't know what I'll do if they send her to jail."

"Maybe you should have thought of that before you let her fill your gas tank for you," she retorted, but instead of turning to leave she sank down on the wooden bench just inside the door. She rubbed her eyes, trying to clear her head, and stared at the floor. "I can't afford a lawyer," she told Harlon.

"But Mariette said you had some money saved," he protested.

She did, but it was money for her future retirement. She realized that to Mariette the money was as good as her own. No, she told herself, she couldn't use the only security she had no matter what kind of trouble Mariette was in this time.

"Aren't you going to do something?" Harlon finally asked after she had sat silently for so long that he was fidgeting beside her.

Mari gave a sigh of resignation. "Yes," she said, standing. "I'm going to swallow the last of my pride." Shooting him a dark look, she advanced on the desk sergeant. "Is there a public phone where I could make a toll call?" She glanced at his name badge and added, "Sergeant Stanley."

"I hope you don't mind my asking," the sergeant said, "but do you have a twin sister?"

Mari nodded. "Mariette Lamott."

The sergeant was beginning to smile. "And you wouldn't happen to be from Pigeon Nook, would you?"

Mari nodded. "Yes, but I don't understand—"

"And you wouldn't happen to know someone named Patrick Keegan?"

Mari chewed her lip. "Well, yes. He's a massage therapist there."

The sergeant chuckled. "I just bet he is. Here, Miss Lamott, you go ahead and use my phone. I wouldn't miss this call for the world."

The drunk stood and wobbled toward the desk. "Are you calling me a cab?" he asked with slurred speech.

"Sit down, Anthony," the sergeant told him. "Your ride's not here yet."

When Patrick answered, Mari was still puzzling over the chuckling sergeant. "Patrick?" she said hesitantly. "Please don't hang up. I need your help."

There was a momentary silence, then gruffly he said, "About time."

"I need you to come to—"

"The Masonfield police department," he finished for her.

"Yes, but how did you know?" She glanced again at the sergeant who was grinning broadly.

"Never mind that. I'm leaving now."

The sergeant looked at the clock when she hung up. "How about a cup of coffee, miss? I want to be wide-awake when he gets here."

Mari didn't understand any of this, but she was too tired and worried to press for answers now. She would wait for Patrick and then hope that whatever influence he seemed to have in Pigeon Nook would extend over here.

The drunk was weaving his way to the coffee machine, and Mari envied him his drunken state. Most likely he wouldn't remember tonight when tomorrow came.

It was exactly forty minutes later when Patrick walked through the door, and Mari thought he looked so wonderful that she didn't worry about the speed laws he must have broken to get here that fast. He took one look at her and was immediately at her side, curving a protective arm around her shoulders.

"What are they charging you with?" he asked.

"Me?" she said in surprise.

"Let me step in here a minute," the desk sergeant said with a twinkle in his eye. "I'm Sergeant Del Stanley, and I believe we've spoken on the phone before."

"Yes," Patrick said, looking from him to Mari. Harlon shuffled his feet in the background, clearly uncomfortable.

"And you're Detective Sergeant Patrick Keegan?" the sergeant asked.

"Detective sergeant?" Mari repeated, staring at Patrick. "I didn't know the YMCA gave out officers' titles."

Patrick looked decidedly uncomfortable. "I'm not really with the YMCA," he said in a low voice. "I'm a cop."

"A cop!" Mari stepped back from him. "You lied to me!"

"*I* lied to *you?*" Patrick said, his voice rising. "I'm not the one who pretended to run a nice little music shop and do volunteer work for seniors while I was over here dancing buck naked on tables!"

"What?" Mari turned white, then pink. "You think I—"

Sergeant Stanley held up his hands. "Hold on here a moment. I think I can clear things up. Sergeant Keegan, may I present to you, Miss Mari Lamott, whose twin sister, Mariette, is at this moment a guest of our fair facility?" He stood back and watched in satisfaction as confusion and then dawning crossed Patrick's face.

"You mean, that was your sister who got arrested?" Mari was nodding numbly, chewing on her lip.

"The traffic charges, the parking tickets, the dancing, all of that?" he asked, and Mari continued to nod.

"Why the hell didn't you tell me that?" he demanded. "Do you know how crazy you've made me for the past four weeks?"

"Wait," Mari said miserably. "You don't know everything."

Patrick braced himself. "All right. Tell me the rest."

She took a deep breath. "My life as you know it is a lie. I've never been past the Indiana border. All of those magnets on my refrigerator are gifts. And I was never a psychic. I was taking Mariette's place after she ran the ad. And I hate alcohol. I pay all my bills on time, I separate my clothes before I put them in the laundry and I even put money in expired parking meters. I'm not exciting or impulsive or the least bit knowledgeable about sex or anything else. I'm dull and boring." She dropped her eyes. "And I don't own a zither."

"Sweetheart, you don't know how glad I am to hear that," Patrick said, pulling her into his arms again and nearly squeezing the life out of her. "And here I thought you were going to drive me to drink with your sophisticated criminal ways. You don't know how hard I've been working to straighten you out."

He turned her face up to his for a kiss, and for the first time since he'd walked through the door of the police department he smiled, just before he kissed the living daylights out of her.

When she caught her breath, she gave him a worried glance. "But what about Mariette?"

Patrick's smile broadened. "You just leave that to Sergeant Stanley and me, honey. I bet between the two of us we can talk to the judge and work out something that involves a whole lot of community service and some strict guidelines. Why, before you know it, she'll be as law-abiding as you are."

"Patrick," Mari said earnestly, "I know that my life could use a little livening up, and I'm going to work on that. Honest, I am. I can be exciting. You'll see.''

''Honey, you're about as exciting as I can stand right now,'' Patrick told her, brushing her hair back and hugging her to him again. ''I love you just the way you are, and if we never set foot out of the house once we're married, that's just fine with me.''

''Married?'' Her eyes widened, and then she felt a bubble of pure pleasure inside. ''Are you proposing to me?''

''I have to, sweetheart,'' he told her, ''or my grandmother and her gray-haired cronies will take a stick to me.''

''We can't have that,'' she said, laughing and lifting her mouth for another kiss.

The drunk, Anthony, had been hovering just beyond the desk, and now he stepped forward, putting one foot in the air before bringing it down as if he expected to step off a curb. ''I love weddings,'' he said, looking to be near tears.

''So do I,'' Sergeant Stanley agreed. ''And I have a feeling that this will be one to remember.''

* * * * *

FIVE UNIQUE SERIES
FOR EVERY WOMAN YOU ARE...

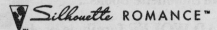

Silhouette ROMANCE™

From classic love stories to romantic comedies to emotional
heart tuggers, Silhouette Romance is sometimes sweet,
sometimes sassy—and always enjoyable! Romance—the
way you always knew it could be.

SILHOUETTE® *Desire*®

Red-hot is what we've got! Sparkling, scintillating,
sensuous love stories. Once you pick up one you won't be
able to put it down...only in Silhouette Desire.

Silhouette®SPECIAL EDITION®

Stories of love and life, these powerful novels are tales
that you can identify with—romances with "something
special" added in! Silhouette Special Edition is
entertainment for the heart.

SILHOUETTE·INTIMATE·MOMENTS®

Enter a world where passions run hot and excitement
is always high. Dramatic, larger than life and always
compelling—Silhouette Intimate Moments provides
captivating romance to cherish forever.

SILHOUETTE YOURS TRULY™

A personal ad, a "Dear John" letter, a wedding invitation...
Just a few of the ways that written communication
unexpectedly leads Miss Unmarried to Mr. "I Do" in
Yours Truly novels...in the most fun, fast-paced and
flirtatious style!

Available September 1998
from Silhouette Books...

That Mysterious
Texas Brand Man
by Maggie Shayne

The World's Most Eligible Bachelor:
Man of mystery Marcus Brand, a
Texan with a wicked grin and a
troubled past.

Crime fighter Marcus Brand was
honor bound to protect a brave
beauty. He never dreamed that his
duty would bring him back to Texas, forcing him to
face the mystery of his past, and the true feelings in
his hardened heart.

Each month, Silhouette Books brings you a
brand-new story about an absolutely
irresistible bachelor. Find out how the sexiest,
most sought-after men are finally caught in...

Available at your favorite retail outlet.

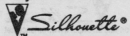

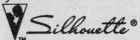

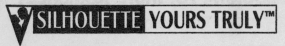